PENGUIN BOOKS

A BREATH OF AIR

Dorothée Letessier was born in Lagny, France, in 1953. After finishing her *baccalauréat,* she worked in Paris as a secretary. From 1976 to 1980 she was a factory worker in Saint-Brieuc in Brittany. It was during this period that she conceived and wrote *A Breath of Air.* Her second novel, *Loïca,* was published in 1983.

Matthew Ward is a poet, critic, and translator. He has translated works by Roland Barthes, Colette, Georges Bataille, Bernard-Marie Koltès, and Pablo Picasso.

DOROTHÉE LETESSIER

A BREATH OF AIR

Translated by Matthew Ward

PENGUIN BOOKS

PENGUIN BOOKS
Viking Penguin Inc., 40 West 23rd Street,
New York, New York 10010, U.S.A.
Penguin Books Ltd, Harmondsworth,
Middlesex, England
Penguin Books Australia Ltd, Ringwood,
Victoria, Australia
Penguin Books Canada Limited, 2801 John Street,
Markham, Ontario, Canada L3R 1B4
Penguin Books (N.Z.) Ltd, 182–190 Wairau Road,
Auckland 10, New Zealand

Originally published in French under the title *Le Voyage à Paimpol*, 1980.

Translation copyright © Viking Penguin Inc., 1985
Copyright © Editions du Seuil, 1980
All rights reserved

This translation first published in Penguin Books 1985
Published simultaneously in Canada

LIBRARY OF CONGRESS CATALOGING IN PUBLICATION DATA
Letessier, Dorothée, 1953–
    A breath of air.
    Translation of: Le voyage à Paimpol.
    I. Title.
PQ2672.E8337V613   1985   843′.914   84-1170
ISBN 0 14 00.7657 3

*In all simplicity, my thanks to Jean-Pierre Barou,
who made this book possible.*

Printed in the United States of America by
R. R. Donnelley & Sons Company, Harrisonburg, Virginia
Set in Primer

To the women workers of Chaffoteaux

TRANSLATOR'S ACKNOWLEDGMENTS

My thanks to Jean-Jacques Sicard, Katia Lutz, and Brigitte Szymanek for helping me hear Maryvonne's voice.

My special gratitude to Irene Ilton for her expert assistance every step of the way. She made this translation possible.

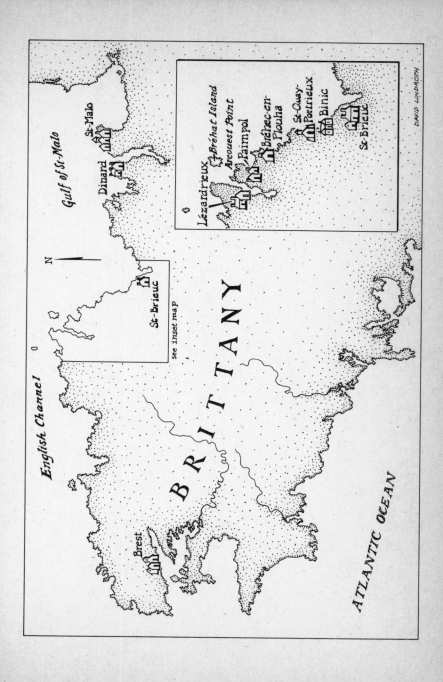

English Channel

Gulf of St-Malo

St-Malo

Dinard

St-Brieuc

See inset map

N

BRITTANY

Brest

ATLANTIC OCEAN

Lézardrieux

Bréhat Island

Arcouest Point

Paimpol

Bréhec-en-
Plouha

St-Quay-
Portrieux

Binic

St-Brieuc

DAVID LINDROTH

A BREATH OF AIR

CHAPTER ONE

"I'm suffocating. I'm going out
for a breath of air. See you.

Love, Maryvonne."

I wonder if I should've left that note on the table. Actually, I
don't have to explain anything to anybody. But I do! We live
in the same house, work in the same place, sleep in the same
bed, we even have the same kid. We owe each other at least
that much. I wouldn't like it if he left without telling me.

Maybe I should have explained more of what I was feeling.
The problem is, I don't even know myself. All I know is I feel
smothered by him. I need some breathing room. I'm only allowed to feel what everybody lets me feel, grudgingly. I've lost
touch with my feelings. I feel like nothing, like no one. Even
my anger has to be timed for everyone else's convenience. At
the factory, I say I can't take it till five! But I behave myself,
like a good girl. Inside me, I hate every piece that comes down
the line, and they just keep coming at me, day after day.
There's no end to it. It might as well be the same piece every
time. I add my part, stick in four screws, and tighten a bolt.
Never the last one. Parts going who knows where, they don't

mean anything to me but cut fingers. I despise them. But I control my anger. Still, it's there inside me, alive and kicking. I keep it caged up. I tame myself. I only get a little moody, or miffed now and then, when what I'd really like to do is scream. I would like to let out my sweet anger and watch it flare and grow. I can feel it about to burst out, red hot and glowing. I gorge myself with rage. I have it in for everybody who keeps me in line. My hate is huge, immeasurable, it out-strips me, rocks me in its arms, whispers bad words to me. Fi-nally, I dare to lash out, and my anger is delicious.

None of them, not even my husband, knows what I'm ca-pable of, me who wouldn't hurt a fly.

At first he'll think I was just feeling a little down, that I've gone out to walk it off, and that I'll be back in time for dinner. He'll think, "A little walk'll do her good. She'll look better and be in a better mood." It'll give him a chance to read the paper and sip on a beer.

Then he'll feed the kid and tell him, "Mommy'll come give you a goodnight kiss in bed." It won't bother him until he notices it's already six-thirty and I'm not there fixing his dinner.

I should have added, "P.S. I won't be coming home to-night."

And what if I do?

I'll look like a real jerk.

He'll be waiting for me. Calling our friends to find out where I am. After a while, he'll think something's happened to me, that I've had an accident, that I've been kidnapped, or raped or something. It's been dark now for quite a while.

I like thinking about him alone and upset like that, won-dering what I'm up to. It serves him right. Let him sit up and notice I'm not there anymore. When I am, he acts as if I don't exist.

I've been whisked away by a naughty little imp, a mischievous genie has spirited me off. My husband, so small, so far away, doesn't know what's going on. "Where could she have gone? I was sure I put her right over here, between the cupboard and the sink, but I can't seem to lay my hands on her. It's incredible!"

He should thank me for spicing up our life a little. I'm treating myself to a little trip, solo.

I slip out of the house without saying where I'm going, and without a shopping bag. What nerve!

I'm abandoning him, with his son and his problems. And I like it. Maybe it'll shake him up a little. He's not considerate enough, and he's too self-centered. He blows up over every little thing and when I need encouragement he's never there.

It's not his fault. There's the factory and money hassles, he's tired and his nerves are shot. I should be more understanding. I just can't be the one to understand everything all the time. I already have one full-time job.

Another two minutes of this and I'll start feeling guilty. I'm the one who gets to him. It's all my fault. I just don't know how to cope.

But all that's going to be different today . . . I'm going for a ride.

I caught the bus at the station, and now, twiddling my "Saint-Brieuc—Paimpol—45 kilometers" between my fingers, I move up the coast, melancholy in the rain.

The bus stops everywhere. It takes close to two hours to go forty kilometers. But it doesn't matter, I'm not in any hurry and I can't back out now.

I look at all the new houses on their nice little plots of green grass. All of them the same, or almost the same, white and heavy-looking under their slate roofs, windows framed with dark stones, granite doorsteps. The chintz curtains open now and then. A woman in a dingy bathrobe appears. She stares blankly at the road. She's disappointed every time. Nothing ever changes. Nothing ever happens.

Some accident, a child falling off a bike, might give her an excuse to go out, to speak to someone. The bread man was by this morning. She bought her daily bread. She ran into her neighbor who was doing the same thing.

"Cold enough for you?"

"What a winter! I sure hope we have a nice spring after all this."

"Well, we certainly deserve it!"

End of conversation. Spending too much time with the neighbors can get you into trouble.

I can just see it—the flowered wallpaper, the scuffs behind the door so that people won't track up her shiny floors, so shiny you can see your reflection, just like on TV. She wanders around her rustic-modern living room like a browser in a furniture store. Her installment-plan living room, just as nice as anyone else's, precious to her as a childhood dream, is ready to receive imaginary guests. Most of the time, so as not to get things messy, she entertains in the kitchen. Set on a lace doily, a crystal ashtray, a wedding present, sparkles in the middle of the coffee table. The thought of putting anything as crude as the ash from her cigarette in it doesn't even cross her mind, and she retreats to the kitchen where the radio is droning on. She's got to stop dawdling around. She's got work to do. She fills the washing machine with laundry that's not even dirty and pushes the button. Then, grabbing her scrub brush and floor rag, she starts washing her hard vinyl floor of simulated red Mediterranean tile. She thinks of something else.

On the bus there are a few women, an old man, children who get on, go a few kilometers, and are let out at a dirt road or at the entrance to some little village.

I feel so out of place that it seems strange to me that all these people get on and off the bus, very naturally, going places, just like that, without asking me any questions. Nobody pays any attention to me. Nobody says, "You should be at work, you should be at home." Shh! I'm traveling incognito.

The windows are streaked and dirty, making the countryside look even more gloomy in the rain, almost unreal. I know this countryside so well: the gray sea you notice every now and then, the dark grass, the scraggly gorse along the roadside; yet it's as if I were seeing it for the first time. I'm only here by chance. And Brittany, struck by winter, silence, and solitude, becomes a backdrop that's lost its soul. The country around here is so sleepy, so restful. All this green. I don't see what's so spooky about trees without their leaves. Their silhouettes are still recognizable, vulnerable, ordinary, quietly outlining the fields and roads.

The stone houses, old and worn, slump on the sides of the road. Their slate roofs, covered with moss, droop down to the narrow apertures, their one adornment, decorated with Brittany shutters painted blue, and peeling. Inside, people grope their way around the one room where the faint light falls across the concrete floor and the heavy furniture. Old women in slippers hibernate, crocheting their lace. From the corner of the window they keep watch over the world that goes from their door to the road.

Beyond that, their gaze is lost in ribbons of mist. What lies beyond the fog?

Paris, Piccadilly Circus, Manhattan. The urban spectacle unfolds before my eyes. I flutter from shop windows to neon lights, from outrageous pedestrians to flashing billboards So thrilled by what I see, overwhelmed with light and magic,

I disappear into all the commotion and become a bus stop, an empty beer mug on a zinc bar, an oily trickle in the gutter, or the tinted glass of a taxi's windshield where the glinting reflections from the street stream by. Invisible. Unconscious. I am the discrete, single diamond in the left ear of some ridiculous man. I'm a little drop of clear polish on the short nail of a young girl. Useless. Superfluous. Delicate.

The driver looks at me in his rearview mirror. I look away, embarrassed. No one else has gotten on for the last few kilometers and I'm alone in the bus. Maybe my little flight of fancy shows on my face. I feel caught in the act. No one's supposed to see me. I'm not here.

It feels so good just to be sitting down. One by one I can feel my muscles relaxing. I don't hurt anywhere. I can cross and uncross my legs or let my arms rest at my sides as long as I want. I open and close my hands. A nail broken to the quick reminds me of the shock, but the pain is gone. My skin envelops me without binding me, without tightening up. I can feel it relaxing, beginning to breathe again. After being clenched against pain for so long it expands with long, deep breaths. On the line, at the machines, even if there's a wooden or metal stool to sit on, you're always tensed up. Your body cramps from all the abuse. Frozen into the one position that's the best compromise between the pace and the discomfort, our muscles, our nerves become one with the hardness of the metal and the speed of the machines. Sometimes you don't know anymore if it's the machine that's driving you or you who's driving the machine. Everything goes like clockwork. You end up not even knowing why you're so worn out.

The driver isn't looking at me anymore. At the last stop an old woman all in black got on grumbling and complaining. Because of the rain, she was annoyed that the bus was late.

The driver kidded with her.

"Heck, you're so well padded, it'd take more than this to get you wet."

"You poor innocent," said the old woman, "if your mother could only hear you . . ."

I settle deeper into my seat. The knot in my throat that was choking me is gone. I notice that I haven't coughed since I left. Yet my bronchitis was so bad I couldn't even sleep.

When I went to see the doctor to get sick leave because I just couldn't stand it anymore, I exaggerated things a little. I have dizzy spells, my arms and legs cramp up, I don't have any stamina, everything upsets me, I cry over every little thing, I work on my feet all day on the assembly line, the pace is too fast, there's no time to catch your breath, no time to go to the bathroom, and when I go home at night, I have to take care of the house, my son, it's all killing me, do you understand? No, he couldn't possibly. "Maybe you should look for another job." Easy for him to say—but I don't have a degree, or even a skill. A pieceworker here, a pieceworker there, it's all the same torture.

It's humiliating to have to undress, to show yourself in such a bad light, to have to justify with your body the fact that you're sick of the life you're living, that you're burned out, that you'd just like a little peace and quiet. The doctor listens, looks, examines, takes notes. He judges from the loftiness of his learning and from his letterhead stationery whether or not you can have seven lousy days of rest. Absenteeism is a serious social ill, it's a form of stealing from owners, from social security, from the government, from the nation-as-a-whole.

And the "presenteeism," which leaves us half dead, which makes us sick, isn't that just as big a waste?

Fortunately, my blood pressure was low, so I got my little printed form duly signed, in triplicate. I have friends who never miss a day of work because they're too afraid to go to the doctor. If "He" ever decided they weren't really sick enough, they'd die of shame. So, weak and feverish, they come to work. Even more than a foreman or a husband, you can't tell a doctor where to go. It's as if he really does have the power of life and death. As if it were up to him whether we're in good health or bad. As if the body we live in becomes something else, some strange object obeying unknown laws. And if my sickness, my exhaustion, my need for rest doesn't show up in my pulse or my digestion, all I can do is put my clothes back on, ashamed. And then it's fifty francs for the visit, every little bit helps. No one's interested in me. My suffering can't be heard through a stethoscope. I must be imagining things. It's just the usual depression. A few ampules of this, a few drops of that, some pills, instructions to take a multiple vitamin with iron. A hundred francs to the pharmacist, and in a week you're back at it.

I got my sick leave and I felt better right away. Seven days to sleep, read, do nothing, and daydream, and that was enough to lift my spirits up a notch.

My son is with his sitter, as usual. If I kept him at home it wouldn't be a rest anymore. His old man is at the factory. Perfect.

But when his father gets home, he decides that the house hasn't been cleaned up enough, that I could have at least done the shopping. Within two days he turns into the one who works, the one who's tired out, and I'm the one who's just lying around all day, who doesn't even have the kid to deal with, who's not getting enough done. Sure I need rest, but there's a limit, this isn't a vacation. None of it's costing him anything, but my being a woman and not working for a few days is all it takes for me to be turned into the homemaker, the housemaid, the domesticated wife, some stupid woman.

He's jealous of my time off. I'm not working, and by staying inside where it's comfortable and warm, I'm betraying him.

To make up for such cheating, to make him forget about my
pleasure, I'm supposed to produce something, a well-made
bed, a weeded garden, a three-course meal. Otherwise, my
selfish, useless days are a despicable waste.

I become a stranger to him. He has absolutely nothing to
say to me. He doesn't trust my questions and thinks he's
being misunderstood. If I feel like talking or laughing or
going out, it's suspect. So I'm supposed to justify my time off
by walking around looking like death warmed over, and by
enjoying my unlawful, guilty time out on the sly. I'd have to
stay in bed all day smelling of formaldehyde or actually be
hospitalized to redeem myself in his eyes.

I'm so tired.

But there's no such thing as tired. The man down at Social
Security scrutinizes my pale face and my prescription. I can't
just up and leave the house whenever I feel like it. I should
mail in my papers within the allotted time. Watched, controlled, I'm under constant surveillance. My house arrest
shouldn't give me any wild ideas. These days off are granted
to me as a reprieve, simply so that I won't go and injure myself on the job by passing out in the bins. It wouldn't look
good. Daydreaming is forbidden. Forgetting about the factory
is forbidden. I end up with bronchitis and cough up my re-
pentance.

The bus bumps along the roads rutted by the ice. I like not
being anywhere. If I'd been a little richer I'd have taken the
train to Paris. For four hours I'd have lived suspended beneath the upside-down reflections of the other travelers in the
Plexiglas luggage rack.

Everything's possible. For once no one's expecting me. I
don't even have to arrive if I don't want to. It's a completely
. . . how do you say, gratuitous gesture, a completely gratui-

tous trip, and I'll never be able to congratulate myself enough for having taken the first step. The arrival doesn't matter and what I leave behind grows paler and paler in the rain with each kilometer.

Now I'm getting somewhere. My life without me is a freeze frame I look at through a two-way mirror. Maryvonne falls asleep and passes through the looking glass. Maryvonne in wonderland rides toward Paimpol. The others are still back there, going on mechanically with their humdrum existence without noticing my absence, without suspecting that my vantage point has changed. The scenes repeat themselves over and over but the curtain, stuck above the stage, never falls. I walk out of the theater. And what if I never go back?

Here I am riding along between heaven and earth and neither means a thing to me.

I'm traveling on the Trans-Siberian Railroad. Moscow–Vladivostok in seven days and seven nights. Nothing to see outside the windows but strange forests for hours on end. Taiga . . . Taiga . . . Taiga . . . Taiga. Seven days without leaving the narrow compartment furnished with all the elegance of a bygone era. Seven duty-free, work-free, talk-free days. Chilly despite my opossum cape and my toque of silver fox pulled down to my eyes, I am the mysterious lady of leisure, without a past, without a country. For a gorgeous Bolshevik, with green eyes and a warm heart, I cross the empire with final orders from the great Lenin hidden in the embroidery of my lingerie on the eve of the revolution. Beautiful as dawn on the steppes, betraying the despised exploitative class for the power of the soviets, Maryvonne Kollontai travels baggage-free.

Seven days to invent and reinvent myself, to explore my runaway imagination. Without living any of it. Without jeopardizing my dreams with any attempt to make them come true. But I'm too old to just take off without having second thoughts. If worst comes to worst I can leave my husband civilly, change jobs and cities, and keep my dignity by keeping my child. What good would that do me? I know myself, my son, my fear of the unknown. I'm not brave enough and I have too many scruples. I feel attached to my life, to the things I love, even though I feel strangled by the tight hold they have on me.

To my son most of all. My son, my alibi, my little entanglement. My ticket into the adult world. My son, whom I've depended on ever since he was conceived, is just a little boy like millions of other little boys. He makes me responsible, he demands that I be there for him. I'm his mother for life, but he has other loves to live. The best that can happen is that we'll listen to each other, respect each other. But the specter of an impossible intimacy will always be there. My son is so handsome, so blond, laughing, and quick. "Mommy! Mommy!" I turn around, it really *is* me he's talking to. Okay, little man, let's say I'll be your mommy.

I'll always be twenty-four years older than him and I'll be the one he turns to for advice about first love and first loss. Our roles are fixed, written forever in time. He's a living being. I won't ever be his wife or his daughter. My autonomous child will never live up to the original orgasm.

Inevitable fate of every generation. Someone's daughter myself, I repeat the offense, I admit my mortality by giving birth when it's my turn. I'm nothing but a moment, a mommy, a mummy. I identify with time, daughter, wife, mother, dead woman. My little boy is a future that doesn't belong to me. Women who say, "My children are everything to me," scare me. I don't want the kind of motherhood that leaves a bitter aftertaste. Let's love and talk, each with a life of his own.

My son didn't choose me. His father is the one who pre-
ferred me, however little, over the others. And I want him to
choose me all over again every day. But there I am, next to
him, plain and handy as can be. I feel like such a fool. I'm too
much and I'm not enough for him. There's so much between
us. We're part of the same family, practically siblings, almost
incestuous. We're too much alike and every day is like the
next. The factory has even stolen our Sundays from us.

He says, "I hate Sundays." Sunday is the day before Monday and you're already in mourning over the coming week.
You're still tired, the hours go by too fast, you don't dare do
anything anymore, and you end up bored to death. I'd like to
enjoy Sunday mornings when the alarm doesn't go off, and
Sunday afternoons when you can see the sky. We could jump
for joy, blow bubbles, explore the center of the earth, or take a
trip in a balloon.

But it's just hot air; Sunday isn't for daydreams anymore.
My Sundays don't mean anything anymore. I feel so alone. I
walk up to him, to touch him, to kiss him, to say something to
him. He pulls away. I'm bothering him. I'm shattered. I try
not to let my eyes settle on the man who's waiting behind a
detective novel for Monday to come, and I fight back this incredible urge I have to cry and smash everything in sight. I'm
either a bored, silly teenager or a nagging frump. I don't
know what I am. Yet I do the factory bit too, I class struggle, I
unionize, I have friends and interests of my own. I guess he
figures I don't have to be persuaded or seduced anymore, it's
one less job for him to do. "Stop complaining, Maryvonne. I
mean, what's the point. Let's make love. Tomorrow's Friday,
everything'll be all right." Yes, every Friday you hope and
every Sunday you're disappointed.

We never make love on Sunday night. In our minds we're
already at the factory. Our throats start to close up. We're

afraid to move a muscle, afraid of making the time go by faster. But nothing works, the alarm goes off and it's Monday morning. Sometimes, out of rage, we fuck.

The factory whistle blows at eight on the nose. I'm at my workbench. The tools and the machines are about to come to life. The waiting is over. Suffering is now obsolete. I'm going to stop thinking and start producing. I feel the slightest little burst of joy run through me. Nothing's bothering me anymore. He's back at it too, in a different shop. Now we can both shut up.

Sometimes I wish I could get at him with a big lie. I'd like to say, "On the way to the store I stopped in at the travel agency. They had this special deal on Greek cruises so I reserved two places for us. Yeah, no kidding, it's true. I put down a deposit. Isn't that great?" No. He doesn't like to go on trips, he doesn't see "the point." Or else I could tell him, "Honey, I have something important to tell you. You remember that journalist who interviewed me during the strike, you know, Jean-François, he was really a nice guy. We saw each other again . . . we ran into each other in town, we talked and we ended up making love."

He'd go, "Hm . . . ," half-resigned, half-upset, and I'd be sorry it wasn't true. Whenever things aren't going well between me and him, all men get on my nerves. I don't want to have anything to do with any of them, not even Jean-François.

Mulling over dark thoughts on this bumpy old bus takes all the fun out of it. I'd be a lot better off making the most of my stolen time off.

We get to Paimpol. That's funny. Just where I wanted to go! Paimpol, it sounds make-believe, like an operetta. Pain-Pôle,

Pin-Paule, Paimpol, a round-sounding word, impossible to whisper. That song, "The Girl from Paimpol" . . . Paimpol and its cliffs . . . the smell of hokey folklore makes me chuckle.

Paimpol means nothing. I don't lug around any mythological baggage about it. I don't get any cheap, nostalgic thrill from this little seaport in Brittany. I like my coast as it is, struggling against oil slicks and other accidents at sea.

Brittany turns whore in the summer, hustling tourist money and selling itself to developers and hucksters. Nobody's perfect. Too often the young people leave. But the stubborn (as the saying goes), less typical Bretons fight against nuclear-power plants. Women who have taken off their lace coifs are demanding the right to work in electronics and other fields. Some women, obviously not very good Catholics, aren't willing to risk death or prison for an abortion anymore. You hardly ever see Breton hats in the streets now except on pardon days and traditional holidays. There are fewer and fewer fishermen in Paimpol, but you still see wooden shoes and blue-and-white-striped sailor sweaters. In the cafés, which have been remodeled to look like pubs, the jukeboxes play disco music. The bombards and bagpipes will come out for the Saturday night *fest-noz.* There are people who just live in Brittany too, and except for a few loafers, tradition isn't an everyday affair. What has to be defended in the streets today is the right not to be isolated, the right to take a train that runs near your house and stops in out-of-the-way places like Plouaret. Today the old railroad tracks are overgrown with weeds, there are no more milk trains, and the dark, empty little stations stand idle. Not so long ago a train used to run along the coast, nice and slow, giving its passengers time to enjoy the sight of the artichoke fields spilling over into the sea. The old-timers tell how you could pass the old train just by running, and how when going uphill, everybody got out of the cars to push the little train that couldn't.

Maybe Brittany isn't any prettier or any purer than any-place else, but I still love it, despite its blemishes and its moodiness. I live between the beach and the woods, between the factory and the little towns where everybody knows everybody. I love the smell of cabbage in the houses, and the pork the people eat sitting around their tables always covered with an oilcloth, and the sausage rolls wrapped in butcher paper. I like the clipped speech, the not-always-innocent curiosity of the people who live here, far from fashion and fads, preoccupied by their own problems, tending their gardens while despairing over the fact that it's too hot or too wet. But I can't stand the cheap wine that leaves the men bleary-eyed. Minds bogged down with "the way it is" and "I heard that so-and-so . . ." give me a pain. I can't get used to this lethargic, temperamental climate. It's always overcast, it never really warms up, and there's always the strange winds and tides that can never make up their minds.

It's out, it's low tide right now. The bus stops at the harbor. I get out. I can do whatever I want. It's weird and wonderful. I don't have a watch, but who cares? It looks like the rain has stopped. The sky hasn't cleared up, but so what? It could be raining cats and dogs for all I care, because today the seasons are all in my head, and my body is immune to the elements.

It's stupid the way my moods depend on the barometer. From now on that's going to change. I'm going to rise above the gloominess, the rain, the oppressive fog, the dizzying wind. I'm not going to torture myself with them anymore, and that's a promise. There are more important things than bleak winters and dreary springs.

I walk along the harbor taking long, deep breaths. I inhale the salt air, which spreads through my whole body. I'm sure a brisk walk will do me more good than all the medicine I've been swallowing for the past week. I've stopped taking it and

I feel better already. The only thing is that Social Security doesn't reimburse you for fresh air. In fact, it's forbidden, since you're barely allowed to set foot outside your house. It's absurd. Staring at four walls can't be the cure for physical and nervous exhaustion. Yesterday I didn't have the strength to vacuum the living room and this afternoon I feel like I could make it from Brest to Paris on foot.

Colorful fishing boats, flat-bottomed rowboats, all the *Saint*s and *Marie*s huddle together. Now and then, in bad weather, some of the smaller boats are lost, but the tragedy doesn't go beyond the family anymore. No more national fund drives started by Pierre Loti, in the *Figaro*. The boats are all insured, and the condolences received by the widows are answered on the obituary page of the local edition of *Ouest-France*. The harbor is crammed with pleasure boats anchored to metal pontoons. The panting motors of the working trawlers, with their exhaust and their loud engines, annoy the people on the sailboats. All they do is cast off, set sail, and let the wind do the rest. I love to listen to the maritime weather reports: "Fisher, Dogger, and Fladden . . . Force 3 to 4 . . . Seas calm to slightly choppy . . . Southern Brittany . . . Northern Ireland . . . Currently no gusting winds, none forecast . . . Anticyclone in the Azores . . ." A long poem filled with millibars and pressure gradients. I purr with pleasure in the gentle summer swell. I sail toward the Galapagos, *tranquillos*. I've left the wife and kid on shore. I'm free. I feel like one hell of a guy and I go with the flow. But that's not right! *I'm* the wife. And a wife doesn't just take off like that, or, if she does, it's with another man; and she always leaves her husband an address where she can be reached in case of an emergency: "Theresa Popinot, General Delivery, Honolulu."

* * *

I'll stay in port . . .

At Arcouest Point you can take the boat to Bréhat Island. If the sky were clearer maybe I could see it. I don't think I'll go. Paimpol is enough, Paimpol and its cliffs you'll never find. I'm not a tourist. I cross the lock that separates the flooded marina from the absent sea. Up next to the jetty the trawlers look ready to keel over at the slightest gust of wind. Imperceptibly, wave after wave, the sea draws closer. I move toward it, but I definitely cannot walk on water, so I retrace my steps with the gulls mocking me with their laughter.

I'm hungry. I'll treat myself to some pastries at that Old French tearoom on the marketplace. There aren't many people. It's not teatime yet, and it's past dessert. The saleswomen-waitresses chatter and carefully arrange the house chocolates, each in its own little gold paper cup, in neat piles. The whole room seems to be made of chocolate and caramel. The varnished wood wainscoting and the banquettes of chestnut-brown vinyl shine like English toffee. The rustic tables and the subdued lighting give a lurid glimmer to the greedy feasting that goes on here. The waitresses walk as quietly as cats and talk in voices as sweet as rock candy. It looks as if I'll just have to have a grenadine soda and a strawberry milkshake. And since I'm not in any hurry, I'll take my sweet time about it. A thin little woman in an impeccable white apron stands patiently beside me.

"Could I have a napoleon . . . and an apple tart . . . and that little cake there, the one covered with almonds, and a cup of tea with lemon, please?"

It's so wonderful and so rare to be eating so much, not really out of hunger but for the sheer pleasure of being here. And such a ridiculous, unhealthy meal—one I haven't even made myself! I am served as if I were the princess of Monaco.

"Could I have another tea with lemon, please?"

The walk, the warm tearoom, and the pastries practically have my head spinning. I stretch out my legs, I close my eyes. Nice and cozy like this, here on the banquette, I could go right to sleep.

"Are you all right, miss?"

The waitress is leaning over me.

"Yes, yes. Just fine, thank you."

I straighten up a little. She called me "miss." Doesn't it show on my face that I'm married? I'm not wearing my wedding ring. I can pass for a "free" woman.

This is strictly a pleasure trip; I have a private income and I don't have to work, or marry.

I keep myself very busy. I travel all over the world, I write articles and poetry. I go to shows and review them for big Paris newspapers. That keeps me in pocket money for stamps and cigarettes, and I give what's left to charities for third-world children and the local poor, and for the promotion of Art and Culture in rural areas. I giggle. The waitress is going to think I'm a crazy woman. I can't really see myself as a rich heiress and I'm not exactly dressed for the part, either. That's the most you could say about my old peacoat.

A woman just walked in. Now, she looks more like who I had in mind. High boots made of expensive leather—at least 600 francs; beige velour pants tucked into her boots to make sure everybody will notice them, and to give herself more of a "sporty" look—250 francs; a thick red fox jacket, poor fox—6,000 francs—open over a soft sweater from Cardin—400 francs. A wide matching leather belt emphasizes her slender waist, the waist of the twice-a-week-for-health lady tennis player—150 francs. A scarf around her neck with the Lanvin logo showing—150 francs. And a shoulder bag from La Bagagerie with a new smell to it—400 francs—filled with elegant, superfluous little accessories. That dame's walking around with four months of my salary on her back. Her hair is done in a natural Scandinavian style, her face is straight out of a glossy women's magazine. She scans the room to make sure everybody's looking at her. Our eyes meet, she is more unreal than a game-show bimbo. Whew! She breathes a sigh of relief—we're not at all alike. She's going to have a little something without any cream or chocolate on it, and tea with lemon, which she'll have without sugar while mentally taking the daily calorie count. She still has an hour before going to pick up her designer child at nursery school. Nibbling at her pear tart, she flips through an art-history magazine they sell at newsstands. She'll be able to talk about the Chardin show at the Orangerie in Paris at the next intimate little dinner party she organizes for the Deputy Assistant from this area. Her husband, who doesn't know anything about painting, will probably contradict her over some date or something, but she'll say, "Michel is so sweet, but he's intimidated by women of culture." And he, a doctor, will respond: "Whenever I hear the word *culture* I reach for my scalpel!" Their friends will find it all very amusing. Then the men will move on to their private beefs with the government.

The young woman who dreams of being splashed up on a billboard in living color: "Do what I do, wear a Kiss Me, the bra you don't know you have on," stands up, leaves a lousy tip and walks out without a word. She would rather live in a big city, and sometimes she feels it's hopeless to put so much effort into her appearance in a dump like this. She doesn't like the fact that she's from Brittany, that her cheeks sometimes get too red, and that she has a slight accent. She wishes she were Parisian, she wishes she knew and, especially, were known by, lots of people. She would go to the theater and go window shopping on the boulevard St. Germain, every day. She could find a job in an ad agency, preferably part-time. Paimpol is too small, there's no way to find a handsome lover for cold winter afternoons. She thinks about the "provinces"

the way a Parisian does. But when she goes to Paris, it's no
use pretending, she always feels as if she has wooden shoes
on her feet and a wicker basket over her arm with a duck
sticking out of it. She's scared to walk down the street, she
gets lost in the metro, she's afraid of being ripped off in the
stores or cruised in the cafés. Nevertheless, she makes a few
purchases at Fauchon without realizing that the aisles of La
Vie Claire are where the action is, and goes back to the hotel
completely exhausted.

My cigarette dies out in the ashtray. What's left of my tea,
in the bottom of the cup, has gone cold. I settle the bill. I
should find myself a roof for the night.

I look for a hotel, like a grown-up. In the narrow cobble-
stone streets, which look like movie sets, there are fishermen's restaurants that smell of hot cooking oil, where they
rent furnished rooms by the day or week. Their names all
have something to do with the sea: the Seagull Restaurant,
the Fishnet, Mariner's Café, the Blue Wave, and so on. The
more modern hotels are down by the harbor.

They're closed for the winter. In the summer, they hire
high-school girls as chambermaids and pay them less than
minimum wage because they're under age.

I go to the Harbor Hotel. An old man in a white jacket is
sweeping the floor of the restaurant. Because of always having to bow his head—toward the ground, the tables, the
plates, and the patrons—his nose hangs downward and looks
ready to droop even further.

The woman behind the desk, her hair up in a tight bun, in-
timidates me. Her nose is buried in her account book, which
is bound in black, just like her. Her dark suit is molded to her
stout figure without a wrinkle. If her mattresses are as hard
as her face, I'd be better off looking somewhere else. Too late,
she spots me and interrogates me in a surprisingly high-
pitched voice.

"Can I help you? If you're here to eat, it's too late, or too early, and we only serve drinks with meals."

"Hello. I'd like a room, if you have one available."

"Oh! A room? Yes, I have a room. Just yourself?"

Why is she asking? Her eyes dart at my left ring finger. No, I'm not wearing a wedding ring, but I'm quite married all the same.

"Yes, just myself."

"You're not expecting anyone? I must tell you right now, after nine o'clock all visitors must be announced."

What kind of stupid rule is that? I've never been to a hotel alone before, but she's making it seem as if it's illegal or something.

"I'm not expecting anyone. I'd like a room just for myself. One with a bathroom, if you have it."

So there! I mean, where does she get off with her police act? I'm not doing anything wrong. And even if I were . . . I'm a big girl! I've got the money, even if there's an extra charge for a woman alone, for a woman without a wedding ring, for a bathroom, for hot water, for cold water, for heat, for a smile on the face of boss woman here.

I asked for the bathroom to show I know what I'm doing, but my budget for this little outing is going to suffer.

"Fine, I can give you number twelve with a bathroom and a view of the harbor. You will be having dinner, won't you?"

I can't refuse, her question is an order.

"Yes, thank you."

"Will you be checking out early tomorrow morning?"

She's really doing her best to discourage me, isn't she?

"No, not particularly. I may be having lunch here tomorrow too."

I try to buy some time. I don't have any idea what I'm doing tomorrow.

"I need to know if it's maybe or for sure."

Why does she hate me so much?

"I'll let you know at breakfast. I haven't decided yet. Is that all right?"

"Well, yes, of course. I'll show you your room. Follow me."

Her lips tighten shut and her whole face sets into a terrible scowl. I'll bet she never smiles.

She's even more formidable from behind. She practically runs up the stairs. The old biddy's got strong legs. I'm all out of breath. Too many cigarettes. She opens the door to number twelve, turns toward me and notices, furious, that I don't have any luggage, not even an overnight case for a nightgown and a robe. A lovely room like this for a woman alone without anything to sleep in . . . well, it just breaks the poor woman's heart. I shut the door and hear her footsteps hurrying away. What a drill sergeant!

The room is bright, despite the ornate, old-fashioned Breton furniture. The floral print curtains match the wallpaper, which is peeling in places. A table is set next to the window precisely for you to write postcards while admiring the view. Love and kisses from Paimpol.

Clean, ugly, shabby, somehow this little room doesn't seem strange to me. Other people, lots of other people have stayed here. Today it's home for me and tomorrow I won't have to lift a finger to clean it. It's as if I were discovering a desert island, a paradise where anything goes because nobody will come, because there aren't any consequences. I have nothing to do. Better than that, there's nothing useful or necessary I can do. Or say. I don't have to explain myself, despite that woman's dirty looks.

I can come and go or just sit around with my arms at my sides, for hours and hours. I don't recognize myself anymore. I'm hidden somewhere in this artificial decor. Find the zebra in this picture. No baggage, no wedding ring, my little whiff of freedom has left me feeling high. I should be at work at this very minute.

At the factory it's already well into the afternoon. I'm dozing off as I work. I wonder what to do about dinner. Forget it. There are still some eggs. I'll cook some noodles and it'll be fine. I watch the hands of the big clock above my head. It's so slow! I swear it gets slower every day. I can't take it till five! I've got to get my quota done. If I want to have time for a coffee break with the others I better speed it up. You're sleeping, kiddo! The others are just like me; they're fed up too, but just how fed up you'll never know. But I do; and it makes me sick, all of it, the work, the foreman who treats us like tools, a salary that's just enough for you to get nowhere. The more time I do in this joint, the more radical I get. Don't laugh! It's true, I'm telling you, you'd have to ditch the whole works and start over, because when you've had it, you've had it! And what about our kids, what kind of life are they going to have with all this unemployment and everything? They'll be treated like animals, just like we are, worse if that's possible. Damn! Okay, I'll stop blabbing now. If I don't I'll end up getting too depressed. So, Maryvonne, you gonna have some coffee or what?

Then it's back to our workbenches. We move like automatons, our voices are lost in the racket of the machines. So we use our wits—we talk without talking, we mouth the words. We make faces, stick out our tongues, wink or smile to communicate with each other despite everything; and often, raising an eyebrow or wrinkling up your nose says a lot more than any words could. At the factory you always feel slightly twisted, and sometimes it's better that way.

The low point of the day comes right after lunch, when it's time to go back. At the company restaurant, across from the factory, the hassled workers file out, shop by shop. Lunch-

times are staggered to avoid overcrowding in the cafeteria.
Everyone always sits in the same place. Opposite me, two
tables away, is where the young workers from the other assembly shop eat. I say "young," first, because they are, and
especially, because they were hired just recently. They laugh
and still believe that "when you've had enough of the factory,
you just get out." There's one I kind of like. He's smooth-
faced and cute as can be. His blond hair curls down around
his delicate face. His blue eyes are amazing, they're so clear.
I've never seen such trusting eyes. He smiles a lot and his
nice straight teeth light up his whole face. There's something
fragile and appealing about him that gets to me. He doesn't
disappear into his surroundings. I stare at him and if he notices, I look away. I have no desire to talk to him. He's just my
own private landscape.

Back with the girls I drink my coffee while it's still too hot,
since there's not enough time for it to cool off. Time's up. I
look at the buildings of blue sheet metal. Smoke rises up from
the stacks. I tell a few quick jokes. We get forty-five minutes
for lunch, and that includes everything. We move as fast and
as automatically during that time as we do at our work stations. Without a watch or a clock we can feel in our bones
when it's time to go back to the grind. If not, the foreman will
start barking at you, and you don't want to go through that
every day. Sometimes, though, you don't give a damn about
the foreman and his three precious minutes, so you stand up
to him. But there are times when you just don't have the guts.
You give in, you go back on time, you put out your quota, you
keep your mouth shut. We leave when the siren goes off and
use our "sore backs" as a cover-up for all the accumulated
bitterness.

The hundred meters from the cafeteria to the locker room
are unbearable. No sooner do I leave and I'm back. Rain or
shine, there's no choice. Despite the sick feeling that comes

over me, I have to go back—four and a half more hours to get through. It's only half past noon. I've worked enough for one day.

"What's with you, Maryvonne, you in a bad mood?"

"Mind your own business. Leave me alone. I don't feel like talking."

CHAPTER TWO

I check out the bathroom, a yellowish sky blue. The big white bathtub looks inviting. The towels are nice and rough, just the way I like them. Laundry softeners are heresy. All the charm of clean clothes is lost in that sticky softness.

Above the old washbasin, with its cracked enamel, is a mirror in a wood frame. I strike a pose. Young woman pensive, sad, surprised, happy. I laugh. Young woman tormented, wicked. I bare my fangs. Flirty, I tease, flip and aloof. My face doesn't look like me. I don't exist anymore. My faces all fade into the mirror one by one. A tired, old, lost-looking woman. How do I look to other people? Looking at myself in the mirror like this, for no reason, I can't even see myself anymore. I'm getting blurry. I'm disappearing. I step away from the mirror. I'm here to have a good time.

I'll take a long hot bath. Too bad if it isn't good for your circulation, as my father says. I won't be interrupted by my kid busting in on my watery realm. I won't have to get out when it's time for the potatoes to come out of the oven.

They say that the function creates the organ, but I only half believe it. If that were true, women would have grown four or five arms a long time ago.

I'm really looking forward to a long, leisurely bath, but I don't want to rush into it. I want the anticipation to heighten

the pleasure. I want to make a ceremony of it. First the tub,
then the solitude, then the time, and, finally, the bubbles.

I'm going to go buy a bottle of bubble bath. I leave the
hotel, keeping the key to number twelve with me. During my
walk I noticed a Monoprix down by the harbor. I always feel
comfortable in stores like that. I've worked in three of them. I
know exactly what it's like. I remember that unreal feeling
they have about them. I was on my feet all day. I was supposed to take care of the shelves—straightening them, putting on price tags—wait on customers, and work the register.
I wasn't allowed to wear jeans. There was this old woman who
used to come in every day; it was her daily outing. It was
warm, and there were people and things and lights. The
muzak and the small talk kept her company. She bought
practically nothing, maybe a spool of thread, a box of pins, a
bar of soap. She liked me because I wasn't as nasty as the
more experienced and burnt-out saleswomen.

One day she brought me a paperback by Gaston Leroux, I
forget the title, and she said to me, "Here, this is for you. You
told me you like to read. So do I, so I thought I'd give this to
you, I hope you like it." She didn't have anything, neither did
I. We became friends. I was so moved that I don't know if I
was even able to thank her.

Immigrant workers like going to the Monoprix too. You
don't have to pay to go in, the lights and the displays are free.

The neighborhood kids spend hours hanging out by the
records and clothes.

They show off in front of the salesclerks wedged behind
their counters. They act cool and play with the change in
their pockets, when they have any.

All of them—the old people, the foreigners, the rowdy
teenagers with sticky fingers—were my buddies. Unfortunately, they were the ones I was supposed to keep an eye on.
I'd be told, "Keep your eyes open, here come some more of

those blacks!'' or else, "Go see what they're up to. Those little
bums've been hanging around the jackets for ten minutes
now." I couldn't refuse; but all I'd do was walk by and smile,
as if to say, "Take whatever you want, I don't care." But most
of the time just the sight of a pink smock moving in their direction was enough to make them scatter, even if they came
right back two minutes later.

Once, two little Arab girls were admiring the perfumes and
the cosmetics in their gold wrappings. The manager yelled at
them, "Don't stand there, you kids. You don't have any
money. Get outta here! Why don't you go take a bath, dirty
little brats!" The poor things ran off, terrorized. But as soon
as the manager was out of sight, there they were again. They
opened a little bottle of toilet water and started rubbing their
faces with it, as if they were washing. The salesclerk caught
them by surprise. She told the manager and in no time the
two girls, in tears, were packed off in a paddy wagon. It all
happened right before my lunch hour. I left the store sick to
my stomach, desperately sorry that I wasn't able to stop it
from happening. I never set foot in there again, even as a customer.

It's because of customers like that, the nobodies who don't
have much money like me, that I come to these stores. I know
what goes on behind the scenes. I know every shelf and the
stone-faced saleswomen, too. I know what mayhem there is in
the poorly lit changing room, always stuffy, where it stinks of
sweat and cheap perfume. I know that the snack room at the
end of the hallway is some little cracker box, and that there's
only one wobbly little table and two or three filthy little stools
to sit on while you're drinking a glass of water flavored with a
drop of some cheap syrup. I can see the time clock and the
metal rack where each girl has a numbered time card, each a
different color depending on work schedule and classifica-
tion. It's rare to be hired full time. They prefer to have part-

time salesgirls for when the store is busiest. That way they don't have employees standing around talking when business is slow. In any case, you can never take it easy, so you straighten the shelves, which is no picnic, believe me, especially in women's clothes. Somebody unfolds one sweater, then another, and another, and then walks off, leaving them in knots. You don't want to leave everything till closing time, so you rush over to refold the sweaters, which are then unfolded again a few seconds later. Over and over and over . . .

At night you have to close out the register, count the bills and the change, roll the coins, the ten-centime pieces with the ten-centime pieces, the francs with the francs. To avoid having to stay past time, you start a little before the doors are locked. That's when some last-minute shopper walks up and wants to pay for a toothbrush with a hundred-franc note. When the bell finally rings at seven, or eight, or ten, depending on the store, it's as if a merry-go-round suddenly stopped spinning. The neon lights are dimmed. The muzak and the ads on the loudspeaker, which you'd become deaf to already, are turned off for the night, and you can hear silence again. The empty cash registers serve no further purpose, their drawers hang open, waiting for the next day. The salesgirls in their pink smocks rush from every corner of the store toward the employees' room. You would never have guessed there were so many. Their voices ring out, "One more down!" "See ya t'morrow, girls!" "So long, everybody!"

The worst time of year for me was around All Saints' Day. I was outside, on the sidewalk, selling chrysanthemums. I never was particularly fond of chrysanthemums, but it was at Monoprix that I really learned to hate them. Big, pale-colored flowers, even coming out of the ground there's something artificial about them. I would wrap them up in cellophane paper. I wasn't very good at it, and the paper would refuse to make a cone, slip off, and fall into puddles of water. I'd staple my finger and the impatient customers would describe the graves of their dear departed to me. The wind would go right through my cotton blouse. To get warmed up, I'd step into the store for a few seconds. The manager would catch me regularly and accuse me of "deliberately leaving the merchandise unattended."

At the time, I was living in a maid's room in an attic, with service entrance and cold water on the landing. It wasn't too bad; I wasn't there much. I was in love, often, and it wasn't any big deal. Whenever these love-friendships petered out, I'd be unhappy for a few days, but it wasn't too unpleasant. I knew it wouldn't last long, that one day I'd have a husband, even a family, and that once swallowed up, it wouldn't matter how many fish there were in the sea. But I tried to convince myself that I wouldn't have to live like all those other twenty-five-year-old fogeys satisfied with their steady jobs, their brats, and their stereos. And here I am traveling forty-five kilometers so I can take a bath in peace!

I buy my bottle of bubble bath. I walk down the aisles. I won't treat myself to a sweater. I only splurge like that on paydays or days when I'm really depressed. On the other hand, I could use a good paperback for tonight. I can never make up my mind when I'm trying to pick out a book. I don't want to hurt anyone's feelings. I'm afraid I'll be disappointed. I'm faithful to certain authors, mostly women when it comes to novels. I pick the one by Christiane Rochefort that I haven't read yet. Too bad it's so short. I like big fat books you can really get into, day after day. Characters you live with for a long time, whom you think about before you're done reading, and whom you run into like old friends in every chapter. I like to lose myself in an atmosphere, in a language that takes me far away. I often feel like talking to the author, writing to her, but I never do because I'm too afraid of being judged and of losing my first response to what I've read. I used to read so much, particularly on rainy Sundays, when I was a teenager, that where the characters' lives ended and mine began always seemed pretty vague to me. I saw my future like a novel, and I wrote my diary with all the solemnity of someone's war memoirs.

Now I'm all set. Walking out of the store I notice that it's gotten dark. Already. This winter is never going to end. I go back to the Harbor Hotel. The big clock says six-thirty, the woman in black has her eye on me and announces, "Dinner is served at seven-thirty. Sharp." Okay, boss, I'll be there.

Once back in my room I take out my new book and stretch out on the bed without taking off my boots, just to irritate the household demons.

Before I start to read, I breathe in the smell of the paper, the printer's ink, the glossy cover. The odor creates an atmosphere of complicity between my eyes and what is about to come to life. I can recognize the publisher by the strong or faint smell of a book. Reading is a physical experience, too. I feel a book, I listen to the sound the pages make. I run my hand over them. I like flipping through them without trying to make out the letters and words, paced by their layout and length. I look at the paragraphs as little paintings, each with its own composition. The book draws its life from the arrangement of its silences, and I breathe in unison with it. It's an obedient companion if it opens, when I want it to, to the right page and keeps me quiet. We spend hours together, days, weeks sometimes, and my moods shift with each line.

When I come to the end of a book I feel both torn and relieved. My work is done. But I've read too fast, and I'm sorry that the ties have been broken. I feel as if the author has let me down by not having anything more to say. Rereading is out of the question, the wonderful surprise won't work twice. Once again I've been fooled, my life hasn't changed. Right away I go looking for another book on which to hang my illusions. I am the heroine of a host of as yet untold stories.

I've already read close to sixty pages. I'm so used to being interrupted when I read, either by people or "better things to do" or just plain fatigue, that I stop automatically. When I was fourteen I could devour three hundred pages at a sitting. I just can't do it anymore. Anyway, I think it's time to go eat.

A quick comb. It's only polite. Standing in front of the mirror on the armoire—I don't trust that other one watching me from above the bathroom sink—and I go downstairs to the dining room. I'm neither early nor late. The clock says seven-thirty on the dot and the landlady appears pleasantly surprised by my punctuality.

Some of the tables are already taken. It hadn't occurred to me that other people might be eating and sleeping here tonight, as if they did it every day. It throws me off. I sit over to the side at a little table set with a white tablecloth. I'm near the bay window overlooking the harbor.

A couple comes in. The man is fat, and ugly, his brown hair streaked with gray. His green eyes flash beneath eyebrows so thick you'd think his mustache was in the wrong place. We're talking seriously ugly. A girl dressed in Parisian mauve is with him. They're having a philosophical discussion I don't understand a word of. Their hearts aren't in it, though, because they're playing footsies under the table. They're probably still in the early stages, when you're still paying attention out of fear of rejection.

I listened to my own sweet-talker once, and it was only when he stopped talking that I started getting old. We'd talk about anything. We'd accidentally-on-purpose brush up against each other. The preliminaries should last for years. I miss the days when we used to take time to hold hands. My husband-to-be would gaze into my eyes, just like in the movies, mostly because he didn't know where else to look. So I took the first step, I was always first. I let go of his fingers with their bitten-down nails, and slowly ran my hands up his arms. My manual laborer's muscles were strong, I liked that, I could feel them hardening under my touch. I'd feel flushed and keep quiet so as not to distract him when he finally decided to take me in his arms and start fumbling with the hooks of my bra. Our nervous gestures maintained traces of efficiency. I wasn't particularly romantic, but just the same, I'd tell myself that one day he would take me to Venice. Later, when I asked him, his answer was, "Venice? It stinks in Venice."

The two lovebirds over there, well bred as they are, get everything off their chests in a hodgepodge of five-syllable words. Their mouths are full of them.

I, on the other hand, have nothing to say. And nobody to whom I can say, simply, "I've had enough," without being given the brush-off. Nobody to listen to me for more than ten minutes at a time.

I should liven up my conversation. I could be sophisticated, even if only once in a while. I'd say things like "You see, my dear, under the present circumstances today, the working class, the proletariat per se, which is to say the laboring, as it were, masses, are, from the viewpoint of phase, which is to say, of period, in political disarray somewhere, in short, all things considered, at an impasse . . . pass . . . passport . . . pornography . . . graffiti . . . fit to be tied . . ." No, it's not my thing.

Jean-François, now he knew how to make me talk! He showed up at the union office one morning during the strike. He wanted to do an article for a newspaper. He didn't know anybody, and I offered to give him some information about the dispute. I was so proud to be on strike! And he was very interested, the workers' struggle was his hobby horse . . .

We went to the corner café. He had big, almond-shaped green eyes and curly brown hair. The romantic gaucho type, but clean. He was a little intimidating. I didn't know where to start. He didn't want to put me on the spot. He said, "Say whatever comes into your head. We'll organize later."

I almost told him I thought he was handsome but he seemed to be pretty well-informed on that score already. I watched him watch me, and my palms were sweating. I started talking real fast. I told him about the strike, the factory takeover, what the workers were saying. He nodded in agreement and interrupted me to describe the future wonders of the power of workers everywhere. Now and then he would ask me if I could be more specific. His eyes would move from my face to his notepad. He was incredibly attentive, sometimes he would finish my sentence before I did. When I felt that I had said all I had to say about the strike, I went on about everyday life at the factory. I told him how for laughs we would sing holding our screwdrivers up to our mouths like microphones. I told him how we play rumor factory, with whatever was initially said being distorted from line to line, to the great amusement of whoever got it going. I told him all about the romantic trysts behind the piles of packing crates. He found it all very amusing. He had put his pen down and it seemed that there, across from me, his face was reflecting what I was saying. He would mouth what I said just as I said it. He'd laugh and start sounding off indignantly at just the right time. I felt so good. He seemed so intelligent. And he was so good-looking. He put his hand on mine and said, "What you've told me is so exciting. If that's what life at the factory is like, I'll go sign up right now."

I was devastated. I was afraid I'd lied. No, the factory is *not* a nice place. I told him about accidents on the job, about people getting sick, the women who can only make it with tranquilizers, the women whose only pleasure is cruelty. I told

him about the women whose husbands beat them and who
hide their black eyes and tears behind sunglasses, those
whose kids "turn bad," and those who can't even cry anymore. I showed him my two-bit disgust and I cried. It got to
him, I know it did. I wanted a little pity, a little help. He
stroked my cheek, gently, and I turned on him. What was he
going to do for me? My little performance was futile and offensive. He wasn't going to work in any factory. He'd write
some stupid article about a strike like every other strike, and
I'd go back to the grind.

I should have told him I like painting, Vivaldi's *The Four
Seasons*, Mayakovsky's poetry, and apple tarts. But that
wouldn't have interested him. I was just a striking worker—
and a likable one—being interviewed. Social conditions, class
struggle, sort of human, Jean-François trapped me. With
pretty eyes and pretty words, but not enough love.

I loved him so much for those two hours that afterward he
couldn't find me again when he wanted to show me his article before it was published.

Life goes on.

Jean-François. I wonder if I ever really met him. The article
is there, all right, in my drawer, but other people could have
told him those things about the strike. I liked sitting there
across from him, but it wasn't really him I saw. I should have
asked him some questions of my own and put some life into
those green eyes of his. It was like being alone and talking to
myself. I treasure the memory. Now I'm alone again. It's so
rare.

It's funny to be eating by myself, without having to get
up between bites, without having to say anything, without
rushing.

Day before yesterday my kid had finished eating and we
were sitting at the table. He was whining because he wanted
me to hold him on my lap. He was hanging on my arm, trying

to climb up on me, stepping on my feet. Telling him to stop
wasn't working, nothing was. His father just sat there. I
couldn't eat. I couldn't stand it anymore, so I gave him a good
shove. He fell on his butt and started bawling. His father
barked, "What the hell's wrong with you! You're crazy! Why
are you making him cry like that? The kid didn't do anything
to you!" I picked him up. Now both of us were crying. I put
him to bed and then went to bed myself.

Incidents like that don't happen every day. Generally,
mealtime is our fifteen minutes for talking, when the televi-
sion or the newspaper doesn't come between us. We talk
about what's happening, about the union, about the factory,
and the friends we have there.

"Did you hear what happened in our shop this morning?"

"No, what?"

"It was freezing. The thermometer barely read forty de-
grees. You could see your breath when you talked. The machines were all frozen. We couldn't work. One woman was so
cold she passed out. Well, we'd had enough and we all took
off to the canteen to get warmed up."

"What did the foremen say?"

"They didn't dare say anything. And it's a good thing they
didn't. Everybody was so pissed off they would have told them
to go to hell. Because they all have heaters in their offices.
That did it when we saw that. They gave us some story about
the boiler being shut down for repairs. But we didn't give a
damn about their boiler. We were freezing, and we weren't
about to knock ourselves out under those conditions."

We also talk about the bills, which never stop coming in,
and about how much we're short. Superficial words for
everyday problems, because to talk about what's wrong with
our lives, to actually come out with our dreams, in words,
could drive us apart. And that's how life is—average, married,
like everybody else. The happy home can't be made into a

novel. Let sleeping dogs lie. But what happens when the poor dog can't sleep? Should he lie?

I left and I'm having a ball.

A man sitting across the room is looking at me, a VIP type accustomed to fine dining. He thought I was smiling at him, and his pudgy face, balding at the temples, breaks into his best public-relations smile. Shit. I look away. Smiling's not allowed. Neither is looking. Or being alone. I put out my cigarette before getting up to leave.

Too late. The super-automatic-blender-mixer-grinder-chopper that beats egg whites and polishes floors is standing in front of me.

"Would you let me buy you a cup of coffee?"

I wouldn't let you do anything.

"No, thanks, I'm not having coffee . . . or tea."

I hope he got the message.

"How 'bout a cup of herb tea then?"

He accompanies his question with a sickeningly sweet smile that means I won't take no for an answer. I resist the urge to laugh in his face. Cruising with chamomile in Paimpol. You'd have to see it to believe it.

"Not that either. I'm not having anything."

"That's too bad. I find you very attractive."

What do I do now? Either I keep quiet and act as if he isn't there or I answer to make it clear I don't want anything to do with his idiotic come-on.

"Sorry, but you see I live with my parents, I've got a glass eye, and I don't come here very often. Now, if you don't mind, I'd like to get by."

The face on young Hoover-Head is quite red. He doesn't like being talked down to, him in his classy, light tan three-piece suit, with a one-year warranty on parts and labor. I bump up against him to get by. I cross the room as fast as I can and walk down the hallway leading to the stairs.

His hand suddenly grabs the banister. Legs spread, he stands on the bottom step, blocking my way. The guy's fast, and persistent. This has gone far enough.

"Let me by!"

"I don't like it when people make fun of me."

"I didn't ask you for anything, just leave me alone."

My face is red with anger now. But it's as if he's getting off on it.

"Come on, come on now, baby, let's not get mad. One little kiss for Daddy. Just one little kiss, that's all."

"Don't you understand French? I'm telling you, leave me alone. If I had a face like yours, I wouldn't show it off in public!"

Score one for me. He thinks he's so irresistible. He stands there a second not saying anything, to calm his rage. I put one foot up on the step.

"Move it!"

"Take back what you just said."

His tone is menacing. Maybe I would have been better off keeping my mouth shut. Now that I've insulted him, I'm afraid I'm in for it. I can feel he has the upper hand. I feel myself panicking here in front of this slob reeking of after-shave.

"Shit!"

Not too eloquent, but it makes me feel better.

"You little bitch, you're just trying to provoke me."

I don't know who's provoking who anymore. His hand, which I never would have imagined to be so hard, is squeezing my arm. Its touch repulses me. I wish I were somewhere else. If I could, I'd call for my defender.

"Say you're sorry with a kiss and I'll let you by."

"No way I'm gonna kiss you, you son of a bitch!"

I won't give in. I'm sick of these guys with divine right who can't think of anything but forcing us to do what they want.

His fist is crushing my arm, my hand is turning white, he's hurting me, the pig.

"Stop or I'll scream!"

I don't like threats, but what else can I do? I'm shaking all over, my mind has gone numb. He's clamped his other hand across my mouth.

I fight back.

He's insane. Help! He's going to smother me. Here, at the foot of the stairs. I don't even know this creep. His sweaty hand is cutting off my air.

"Slut! Slut! Slut! You gonna kiss me? Huh? Yeah, you're gonna kiss me."

I kick wildly, but it doesn't seem to have any effect. His eyes flash with hate: it's the devil himself. But I don't believe in the devil. I'm suffocating. Panic and rage grip my stomach. He keeps slobbering on me. I'm going to puke on his sales-rep suit.

"You're gonna kiss me! You're gonna kiss me!" He pronounces each word mechanically, in a shrill voice. His eyes don't even see me anymore. He's a mad animal. I'm going to die. How awful, my son will miss me. I can see myself sprawled out here on the stairs in a pool of warm blood. What did I come here for? I gasp.

Footsteps. I hear footsteps.

Am I delirious or is it for real?

All of a sudden the grip loosens.

"I'll get you yet, you whore!"

He's gone. The two lovers appear at the end of the hallway. They've saved me without knowing it. Before I can even catch my breath, I run up the stairs. My room! The key trembles. The keyhole's gone. No. There. That's it. I slam the door, turn the lock twice, and start trembling again. I can't help myself from repeating, "It's not fair. It's not fair. It's just not fair . . ."

I don't know if I'm more afraid or angry. That bastard! Who do they think they are? They all make me sick with their slimy paws, their stupidity, and all their hate. They can't stand the fact that we might be able to live without them. I hate them. All of them. They're all the same. They don't even deserve the fear they inspire.

I drink a big glass of cold water. It calms me down. I'm not going to let myself be had. I'm not going to let that filthy pig ruin everything. It's so disgusting, so unfair. Just forget about it. Attacks like that are such bullshit. Men make me feel ashamed to be human. To say that I belong to the same species as them is revolting. Their viciousness humiliates me. I don't want anything to do with them. They won't get me every time, that would be more than I could take.

I'm calming down. I want to live. Me, my life. My trip, my fun. Just for me.

I'm going to take a nice hot bath.

I splash the deep blue liquid into the empty tub, and the gushing water makes bubbles and steam flower up like Japanese blossoms.

CHAPTER THREE

Marilyn Monroe, leaning over her big pink marble bathtub, gazes at the mauve-colored soap bubbles frothing and filling it up. Dozens of opalescent and crystal flasks decorate her bathroom. Subtle perfumes mingle their delicate fragrances in a bewitching bouquet. A diffuse light eliminates all shadows. It is warm. Everything is perfect. Marilyn straightens up. Her white silk negligée slides down her smooth body. She doesn't know anymore whether this is her own home or whether it's the tenth take of some scene from a movie. Just to be safe, she smiles, and avoids looking at her legs as they disappear into the hot water.

Marilyn stretches out in the pink marble tub. Only her face shows above the Hollywood froth. She has no makeup on, her hair is wrapped in a turban.

This really is her own body, imperfect, far away from the camera's eye, her own body dissolving in the bath, her own body drifting away. Eyes closed, Marilyn's smile is gone now. She lets herself go. She can feel the water protecting her, seeping into the tiniest crevices of her skin. She is reunited with her hidden, battered, bartered body. She knows its faults, its weaknesses. She spreads her legs and floats in the gentle, liquid caresses. The hot water is still running to keep the bath at a constant temperature. This could last for hours.

Marilyn vapory. Marilyn voluptuous. Marilyn fleshy, languorous, languid. Marilyn in abandon. Marilyn in ecstasy.

Marilyn doesn't bother with soap. Doesn't scrub herself. She's not in the tub to get clean. This is pure luxury, pure pleasure. A bath of pink marble and purple foam to wipe away pain and fatigue. A scented bath to drown lies in. A place to be sad all by herself, if that's what she wants.

Marilyn farts in the water and watches the bubble rise to the surface and pop with joy in the steamy air. Marilyn giggles. At her next interview, she'll break it to them:

"Dear, marvelous Marilyn, what is the most important thing in your life? Men? Movies?"

"Oh, neither, darling. What I adore most is a good fart in the tub."

She knows perfectly well she can't do any such thing. They'd say, Marilyn is going through a severe depression. The journalists would spread the news around that the luscious Miss Monroe is intellectually primitive and emotionally blocked at the anal stage.

Impossible, too, to say she enjoys pissing in bidets, and that it's all that's left of her childhood with the toilet down the hall.

Marilyn lifts one leg out of the water and foam. A shiver skims across her calf. Little bubbles cling to the hairs on her leg and form white trickles along its curves.

Marilyn has hairy legs.

Marilyn has knobby knees.

Marilyn works on the assembly line.

Marilyn's name is Maryvonne.

And Maryvonne has sagging tits.

It's pregnancy that does it to you. My breasts swelled and swelled. It was phenomenal, especially after I gave birth, when the milk started coming. I had boobs as big as melons. Nowhere in town had a bra big enough for me. The overflow of flesh was so uncomfortable that I didn't know which way to turn in my little hospital bed. Udderly miserable.

Inevitably, when all the swelling went down, the loose skin flopped down to my belly. No big deal. At least I still have nice ears. That's what my grandmother always used to say. I have such pretty little ears. Unfortunately, they're neither productive nor seductive. Who notices nice ears, other than meticulous grandmothers looking for family resemblances on little girls' bodies? I have nice ears and nobody could care less.

I part the bubbles and look at my stomach. Flat. As if it had never been on the verge of bursting. As if no one had ever lived in it. I can feel its quietness, its emptiness.

I liked my huge belly which defied all belts and put its distances between other people and me. The last day of my pregnancy that I spent at the factory, I was very tired, but I didn't realize just how tired. At the corner of one of the bays I didn't move out of the way fast enough when I heard a horn beeping, and I collided, belly first, with a fork-lift, which fortunately wasn't going too fast. I thought, "See, little one, factories hurt you."

My motionless stomach no longer stirs. But the memory of the pain comes back. I was meant to give birth, a noble piece of work, inevitable travail, and not a bit of glory in it. I didn't know what was happening. I had to grin and bear all the miserable torture when I felt like screaming. My labor was not a pretty one. My premature baby and my demented body turned me into another person. With my eyes riveted to the ceiling light, which was blinding me, I kept repeating, "Let me out of here, let me go, I want to get out of here."

I feel pummeled, pounded, terrified. Does something in me have to be destroyed in order for my baby to be born?

Finally, after hours of struggle, I expel my torturer from

me. The wrenching pains are over, things are calm again. All I'm aware of is the joy of not suffering anymore. Self-preservation instinct or maternal instinct? I cherish the birth of my baby. Never again will he be able to cause me so much pain and suffering. Never will I love him as much as I did at the moment I was delivered of him. It wasn't his hand, or his head or his tiny little penis that violated me, it was his whole virgin body, which made love to me on its way, and which took the life out of me, both at once.

And then, my baby, this other person inside me, leaves me and becomes an unknown nursling who drinks, sleeps, and wets himself. I'll never forget that little death, which left a crease of bitterness around my navel.

I curl up in the water. I am the giant fetus with wrinkled hands. I bob up and down. Clean.

My fingertips have finally lost that dirty look they always have no matter how much I wash them. I can't stand having dirty hands anymore, covered with grease and a dusting of copper filings and tiny bits of lead and aluminum. I'm struck by it in the middle of work. All of a sudden I notice my hands and I don't recognize them, they're disgusting, I run to the sink to wash them. I scrub like a maniac. After the soap and cold water they look more red than white. I'm whole again. I dawdle a little in the bay between the machines before going back to my place. I pretend I'm a visitor. What a funny place this is, really, those bowed heads, those busy hands, those faces intersected, like in abstract paintings, by cables and pipes that block your view.

Everything is so severe and complicated that it all seems unreal. You can't see the workers for the machinery, you guess at them from a little hair showing between two machines, or a foot sticking out from under a container. I know whose they are. I know the names and, sometimes, even one or two things about the lives of my fellow workers. I make my way without getting lost in a maze of machines. I'm home. I take up my place again. My hands plunge back into the filth.

Our hands tell the story of our life. During the last strike, the hands of the workers busied themselves in the softness of knitting yarn. Where there had been commotion and noise there was calm and relaxation. Seated on boxes or metal wastebaskets, the women set up house. In the canteen people were playing cards. For morning and evening meetings, everybody gathered in the big corridor in front of the locker rooms. I was so radical I believed everything should change.

I climb the iron staircase to the overhanging walkway above the corridor. Four meters above me, twelve, thirteen, fifteen hundred workers mass, making quite an uproar. An enormous blue wave moves toward the walkway. I know the faces raised toward the microphone. They are attentive, almost serious. The meeting is about to begin. I walk up to the microphone and look way out in front of me, to the other end of the hall, where I can't make out the faces of the strikers anymore. I've written my speech in big red letters so I won't forget what I have to say. The crowd quiets down, they're waiting for me to start. Here I go: "Comrades! . . ." My voice, amplified over the union's PA system, echoes from head to head. I take a deep breath, and in a confident voice I deliver my speech, forgetting my notes: "All of us, men and women, young and old, are united in this struggle . . ." They listen, I'm afraid of saying something stupid. ". . . Not one more piece of equipment should leave this factory . . . organize picket lines . . ." In waves, murmurings pass through the crowd. As I end, my voice rises, ". . . we're the ones who are strong . . . we'll show them just how strong . . . and we're going to win!" Thousands of hands that had been buried in pockets come out to applaud. I look over at my pals who wink at me. You let yourself go and believe that things can change.

We win a few centimes and go back to the same old grind, the same old pace. The strike and its false hopes are lost.

Even more than before, everything is pressure and routine. The machines whose metal cuts at my fingers. The foreman who glances at his watch if I stop a second to say something to a friend.

You start getting up early again, when it's still dark, to make sure you're so dazed you can't even react. I barely make it every morning, sometimes I'm late and once I am, I can relax. If you're going to be late, might as well be good and late. When I finally get there, pretending I'm sorry, I hear, "Hey, Maryvonne, teacher keep you after?"

You end up having a mental clock. Your eyes open right before the alarm goes off, even if you haven't gotten enough sleep. You always eat at the same time, hungry or not, always in a rush, mechanically. A lot of people resign themselves to it and end up saying, "You have to accept what you can't do anything about." I wish somebody would do something!

During the strike, I was in love. He was a worker, too, always ready to smile. During one of our marches, our eyes met. We made our way toward each other. I took his hand. We both felt thrilled by the touch. We stole a kiss in the middle of the singing, jostling crowd. Then we let ourselves be separated again by the flow of strikers. A friend yelled, "Don't blush, Maryvonne, he's your husband!"

I wish men would run out of reasons to shorten the time they give to love and that the dumb would speak. We'd drink rosewater by the glassful!

But I digress. I mean, I'm rambling.

The warm water is making me dizzy. I feel so heavy. I don't have the strength to move. A fugitive factory worker, holed up in the bottom of a hotel bathtub, dies of inactivity. "It was to be expected. The shock was too great. Her heart couldn't take it." I could go to sleep, right here, nice and peaceful, forever, drown and not care. But the water's getting cold.

She's getting chilled.

After a mad dash through the trees and the bushes, which scratched at her legs, Maryvonne reached a lake. The path ended there. She stopped, breathless, and turned around. She had outrun him. Soon, however, she heard the sound of his feet snapping dead branches on the ground. Without thinking, she jumped into the water. She began swimming furiously, striking the water with all her strength. Her clothes, clinging to her body, hindered her progress. But when she turned her head a second time, she realized, as she neared the other side of the lake, that the man had turned on his heels and was going away. He was throwing in the towel. She was saved, this time. The last few meters before reaching shore were agony, a real calvary. She couldn't go on anymore and had to summon all her will to live in order to keep herself from going under. Exhausted, she dragged herself onto the bank, grabbing onto the reeds and, once out of the water, she rested a long moment stretched out lifeless on the grass, face down on the moist earth. Then shivers ran all through her, her frozen arms and legs were trembling. She stood up painfully, stepped over the edge of the tub, grabbed the bath towel hanging to her left, and rubbed herself vigorously to get warm again.

There are white cotton sheets on the bed, a little heavy, rough to the touch. They make me think of the trousseaus young girls had before the war. But I can't really imagine tonight's landlady as a virgin bride.

I lie down diagonally. I have the whole bed to myself. Reclaimed territory where I can stretch out, roll over, turn around, put my feet up on the wall, and leave the light on all night if I'm afraid of the dark. Nobody will interrupt my dreams. I won't be subjected to going through the motions of love without desire. I won't have to fake it. I won't have to disguise screams of rage as moans of pleasure.

I wasn't so cold in the beginning. I wanted him all the time. Nothing else could release all the tension in my body.

The first time I saw him, in his work blues in the shop, in the middle of the line, he was leaning over some assemblage screwing on a bolt with a pained expression on his face. All that was wiped away when he turned in my direction. And, as I was saying "I love you" to him with my eyes, I blushed down to my toes. Affection has no business in a factory. We waited five hours with that terrible longing to be together and forget everything. We held each other so tight we couldn't breathe.

After a day spent in the racket of sheet metal we would listen to one another whispering with rapture. Our swollen hands, callused by the tools, would try to soften and whiten themselves by stroking and caressing the other. We were like those little kids who charge out of school and run into their mothers' arms. Our physical pleasure was only the smallest sign of our collusion. We would talk about all we'd been through and everything seemed to point to our meeting. It had been a long wait, but we found each other, again and again, and we had to make up for lost time and finally start living. Love. Always. Forever. We threw around that naive vocabulary, regretting the fact that it wasn't ours alone. We had nothing to do with the ordinary feelings other people felt. We were special, only we knew how to love. Our clearly predestined meeting left us feeling so full of ourselves.

I would stare at him, he was so handsome, and the sound of his voice gave me goose bumps. I'd brush against him and, like a shot, his warmth would run all through me. We would work miracles. Everything would be wonderful, like our love. For breakfast I would buy two dozen croissants, even if it meant they'd go uneaten and stale.

We made love a lot. There was still more blood than iron filings in our veins back then.

Hell crept up on us with each passing night.

Our bodies separate at six-thirty in the morning and it gets harder and harder for them to regain any feeling come night. I told myself I'd follow him no matter where, but he didn't want to take me anywhere.

I'm cutting out. I flew the coop. My mind is playing leap-frog with reality.

When I go back, and I will go back, everything will be different. He'll take me in his arms and say, "I love you," like in the beginning, with that kind of wild look in his eyes. We'll ditch work for the whole day and use the time to talk and hold each other like before. Some nights, after leaving the factory behind, we'll go look at the sea, so pretty in winter, and he'll say, "I thought about you all day and now that we're together, I'm falling in love with you all over again." I'll be reassured and we can change the subject.

But we don't have the time. We walk right past each other sometimes, we brush against each other without even noticing.

I'm off in another world. I'm playing make-believe. I'm fantasizing. I'm inventing some perfect lover who enters my bedroom, where the luxuriousness of the satin sheets is rivaled only by the silkiness of my skin. He is draped with embroidery, lace, and sequins. His eyes sparkle with glittering gold makeup. And they smile. At me. I sprawl out on perfumed furs and he joins me, catlike in his rustling lamé dressing gown. The jingling of the gold bracelets and precious stones of our words accompanies our sophisticated frolic. My handsome lover swoons with pleasure as he gives his smooth body over to my caresses. He lies motionless and modest beneath my kisses. He allows me to explore his skin inch by inch, and moans softly beneath my fingertips. I run the show. He lies there; his pleasure mounting. Then, with one quick, precise, flashing stroke, like the sharpened silver of the dagger itself, I pierce his chest, clean through to his heart. His face barely quivers. He'll never leave me again. The red stain spreads over his silk shirt, in a ring around the carved dagger. He is mine forever. Truly. A love for love's sake. Not a love you pay for on the installment plan for thirty years.

Alas! It isn't really my style, my century, or my story. Our ways of behaving and dressing are more conventional, on the casual side, and very working-class. Apart from my ears, maybe, I'm no femme fatale and my husband is feeling just fine, thank you.

I take my pill. Getting caught once was bad enough. I always carry my dispenser with me. It's my only indispensable baggage. I don't like forgetting things, being caught by surprise, lapses of memory, the excuses that spoil love's secret little mysteries.

I wonder what he's doing now. Is he lying in bed like me? Is he surprised to be alone? Happy to have the whole bed to himself?

It's still too early. He'll watch TV till it goes off the air at eleven, to keep his mind off the questions that are nagging at him. Then he'll put on a record and try to concentrate on a book and chain-smoke his Gauloises.

In the kitchen, his dirty dinner dishes are waiting for me to get back. He lies still for a minute, staring into space. Then he rereads the pages he just read without realizing it's the third time. He doesn't feel like reading anymore. He throws down the book and decides to go to bed. She'll get here when she gets here, no reason to get all excited. He has to get some sleep. Before going upstairs he checks to make sure there's enough coffee for his breakfast.

Walking into the bedroom he's struck once again by my absence. He would have liked to believe that I had just gone to bed before him, as I often do. But I'm not there asleep under the covers. It's not over yet. He'll sleep alone and wake up alone. He says to himself, if she comes back before I count ten, I'll hold her in my arms, and I'll keep my mouth shut. We can have it out later. He counts, slowly, nine, ten. Nothing. That's life, win a few, lose a few. You can't expect too much. He goes to bed and eventually falls asleep. I'll give her twenty-four hours.

Once you're married, why put yourselves out? I still try sometimes, using holidays as an excuse.

For example, I'll fix myself up for a Christmas Eve party with friends. I want to be noticed. I want to look sexy, I want to be somebody else . . . I want my hair to shine in the light of the fireplace. My body, my movements, my voice are relaxed—no problems, no pains, no punching in. I want my makeup to change my eyes into magic charms in the candlelight, and my face, which he knows like the back of his hand, to look fresh and pure to him. And then the woman inside me would excite him again. I'd be the woman of his dreams, the woman he desires, if that's what I want and if he loves me. Too bad if I need a little makeup to look good, it's not a mask, it just brings out the real me. We'll make love new. You'll forget that my hands are too wrinkled and dry for their age, the cracks and calluses on yours will disappear. I'll be the woman who pleases you, whom it pleases me to invent for you.

If you slip out of the fantasy, if you make workaday love to me, I've failed. The magic becomes a ridiculous getup. There by yourself, the smell of beer and tobacco gives you a different kind of pleasure. My dream is shattered under your heavy sleep. You don't want to know me. All that's left is a queasy dawn and a pretty dress lying rumpled on the floor.

If that happens he won't even notice I'm gone.

Him, who goes out to get a loaf of bread at the corner and comes back two hours later. Everything's ready, he doesn't say a thing, he eats and watches TV. I feel sick to my stomach and go to bed. I'm still not asleep by the time he comes upstairs. When he gets under the covers I'm afraid that if I accidentally touch him it'll make him want to have sex. I don't want any of his dumb, mechanical stroking. I whisper stupidly, "Stop that, I'm asleep . . . stop it, you're making drafts, lie still." His arm stops around my waist, and he falls asleep like his son holding his teddy bear.

Tomorrow we have to get up again, denied both warmth and sleep. Wake when the alarm clock gives the order, just to be cold again. Surrender and hand ourselves over to the factory, something dead inside.

I turn all this over in my head and I can't get to sleep, yet I'm exhausted. I toss and turn. Everything bothers me. I don't have enough room, or air, I have a headache that's getting worse, threatening to make everything explode. I feel like crying, sobbing my heart out, screaming, anything, but I don't dare. I get up and, feeling around in the dark so as not to wake him up, I take two aspirins or a sleeping pill. I tell myself I'm sleepy. My body collapses, my leaden arms and legs dangle in empty space pulling me to the edge of an abyss. I slip. I fall, unable to withstand the force crushing down on me. I don't have any clothes on and my heavy nakedness fills me with shame. I'm so tired. But I'm not allowed to let up. They won't let me sleep, they talk at me, look at me, judge me. I struggle, desperately, to maintain a little human dignity, but I feel more pitiful than a scrap of bloody innards on a butcher's block. I ooze. I trickle. My engulfed will leaves me unable to keep my eyelids open. Everyone, the foreman, the union secretary, my co-workers, my husband, my son, all look at me with disgust. I'm a weakling. I'm nothing but a streak of stinking mud under their feet. They step on me and curse at me as they go by. The others keep spinning and turning like merry-go-rounds and kaleidoscopes that make a noisy rattle. They denounce me. I'm paralyzed. I can't fight it anymore. I'm too sleepy. I'm falling asleep.

The next day my mouth is dry, my eyes swollen, my mind foggy, my movements listless. I drink coffee all day to make my quota and at night I'm too wired to sleep.

One hell of a life!

The worst thing is that even if I had known what was in store for me on the other side of adolescence there's no guaranteeing I would have been able to escape it. I used to believe that this was the life I wanted. Working to make a living, having a man and children at home to love, owning a car and some furniture for comfort and appearance's sake. "Stop biting your nails," my father would say, "if you don't, you'll never find a husband." I did. Maybe I would have been better off biting my nails and becoming a homeless old maid.

You can't pretend like your shit smells any better than anybody else's. Happiness isn't a house pet . . . so what?

Listen, Maryvonne, you're lucky, you don't know what really bad is. Look at Vickie, a widow at twenty-five. Look at Arlette, her son was killed. But that's no consolation, I feel the misfortunes of others as if they were my own.

In the locker room Arlette's face is framed by two metal doors.

She looks haggard and disheveled. Her nose and her mouth are held tight as if to hold back sobs or to brace themselves against others' pity. Her eyes refuse to see. Her dull gaze is fixed elsewhere.

Her grief is unbearable. I'm stunned by it. I don't know

what to say. There's nothing I can do. "Hi, Arlette." I barely manage to stop the unfortunate "How are you?" from slipping out, and head for the shop.

She was out for only ten days. She moves like a sleepwalker. She forces herself to listen to what's being said around her, but a lot of the time you get the impression that the words don't penetrate the sadness that envelops her. Everything else pales in comparison. She saw her son die.

Ten days ago, she was wearing a cheery sweater with pink and blue and yellow stripes, "to entice spring." She was laughing because she loves to joke around. She was telling me some of the cute little things her youngest had been saying. I like her so much. We don't see much of each other now that we work in different parts of the shop. We run into each other in the locker room. In memory of the good times we had on the line together those first months at the factory, we've stayed friendly. Last year's strike enabled us to enjoy each other's company again. When it came to knocking the bigshots down a notch or two, she was the best. Her eyes would sparkle with mischief.

I'm talking about her as if she were dead. She's still alive, but her laughter doesn't ring out in the shop anymore. She's not a widow or an orphan, she's both at once. There are no words for the irreparable loss of a child you brought into the world.

The beautiful Arlette who's clapping and singing in pictures taken during the strike disappeared one Monday in February.

The school bus drops Nicolas off near his house. All he has to do is cross the street. He's twelve. He knows life isn't easy for working people. He doesn't like it when his mother is all worn out and grouchy, and gets all upset when he and his sisters get too noisy. He wishes everything at home could be nice and happy. If only they talked to each other at night after dinner instead of watching TV all the time. But there are more arguments than conversations. He can tell that his parents don't get along like they used to when he was little. Mommy's always in a bad mood. She takes it out on everybody in the house and scolds them for every little thing. But Nicolas knows that it's not just because the toys are scattered all over the place that his mother is unhappy. He wishes he could do something for her. When he gets big, he'll make it all better. Tonight he's hoping she'll be happy when she sees his grade in arithmetic. He tried really hard. He wants to show that when he tries, he "gets it." Pretty soon he'll get a job and make lots of money. He doesn't know what yet, but he doesn't want to work in a factory. He'll always be in a good mood.

Nicolas gets out of the bus first. He hurries to cross the road. He does it automatically, every day, he doesn't even think about it.

The car shot out.

Too fast to stop.

At the last second, the driver slams on his brakes as hard as he can. He tries not to hit the boy. But Nicolas dashes into the car. The side of his head catches the door handle.

He's stretched out on the asphalt. His skull is open underneath a bloody handkerchief laid across his forehead.

Arlette and her husband were notified right away. Nicolas was still alive, the blood streaming down his face. He was taken to the hospital in Rennes.

For three days and three nights Arlette and Nicolas held off death.

Arlette hoped against hope. "Doctor, tell me the truth, is he going to make it?"

The encephalogram shows almost no activity, irreversible

brain damage. His pulse is very faint. He can't live much longer. Arlette tries to convince herself that it's better for him if he dies in peace.

Arlette saw her son's body stiffen in a final spasm. She screamed. She wanted to throw herself out the window.

No! It can't be. It's not true. My baby, my little boy, I love you. I won't get mad anymore, I'll sing, all the time. You'll see. Don't leave me. It hurts too much. I can't take it. Nicolas! Say something, please, please. My son is dead. My son is dead. Dead. What am I going to do? My baby, take my heart, my head, my life, but please don't die! Somebody help me! My baby is dead. Look, here he is, all white on this bed.

Where is the bastard who murdered him? I want him to see what he's done to my Nicky.

Arlette started crying softly, crushed beneath an overwhelming exhaustion. Her husband was crying too. He led her away. They didn't talk all the way home. The other children had been taken to their aunt's. Arlette fell into a deep sleep and woke up, suddenly, in the middle of the night, in a cold sweat, terrified by a nightmare. She dreamt that Nicolas had just died. Her husband, lying next to her, hadn't been sleeping and was choking back sobs. It wasn't a dream. Nicolas had died that afternoon.

Nicolas starts over. He gets out of the bus calmly. Looks right, then left before stepping into the street. There, that's good. Let the car go by. These drivers are crazy, you're supposed to stop behind a school bus. One of these days there'll be an accident. Coast is clear now, Nicolas, you can cross. So, come tell me what you did in school today. Good, you're starting to wake up in arithmetic. You're paying attention now? I'm telling you, Nicky, if you don't know math you'll never get anywhere in life. Look at me, I didn't bother to pay attention and look where it got me. You don't want to be a poor working stiff like your parents, do you? If you do well, it'll give me the strength to go on. That's all there is to it. All he has to do is make it across the street and he's saved. Nicky, why didn't you look where you were going? I told you a hundred times, look both ways before you cross.

Even as a baby you were impossible. You cost me a fortune in Mercurochrome and bandages. You were afraid of the dark. You wouldn't go to bed when you were told, and you'd wake up during the night screaming because of some bad dream. How many times did I sit up all night with you? After all I went through to make sure you'd grow up healthy and strong. Just when you were doing so well in school, and had become such good company, somebody goes and kills you like an insect on a windshield.

I can't bear it.

When Arlette can't go on, when she can't choke back her grief anymore, she runs to the bathroom and lets out a flood of tears. She tells herself that the pain will ease up, it takes time. Other women, women she knows, have been through it. She tries to bind up her wounds in the fabric of everyday life. Sometimes she just wants to forget about it, but the way people look at her reminds her how pale she is, how dark the shadows around her eyes are.

She knows she looks as if she's aged ten years, that she frightens people. No one dares talk to her like before. Everybody's careful not to joke around in front of her. Laughter dies down when she walks by. The other mothers shrink from the pain etched on her face and turn away discreetly out of some superstitious fear of contagion.

Arlette is all alone. Her friends are there, caring, trying to understand. But there isn't anything to understand. You have to go on living. She'll make it. She wants to make it. It'll just take time.

I wanted to tell Arlette how close and how far away I felt at
the same time. But I'm afraid of saying the wrong thing at the
wrong time, afraid of digging up memories she's trying to
bury, and unable to spare her further pain. I feel so awkward
around her. I brood over her sadness and it becomes my own.
Helpless, foolish, I shut up. I get involved in the union. I want
to change the world and I can't even tell my friend that I
share her suffering. I hate myself.

There's too much unhappiness. I'm surrounded by cancer,
accidents, suicides. There's always somebody to cry over. I
don't know what to do with all the tragedy anymore. It makes
my head throb. All this suffering tears me apart. I don't know
if I should blame it on fate or start believing in God. "I don't
want to hear another word about death."

During our break the women read the local news items in
the paper. Then they move on to something else. You can't
spend your whole life crying.

"I'm going to go buy a bed-set at the co-op during lunch. I
want to get those sheets with the floral print."

"Do the bed-sets at the co-op come with fitted sheets?"

"Uh-huh, fitted sheets are so much easier, they don't
come undone and you spend less time making beds in the
morning."

"I don't like fitted sheets. They may be easier when they're
on the bed, but they're so messy in the linen closet. You can
never get them to fold flat, even if you iron them. They make
a mess. I don't buy 'em anymore."

"Not even for your kid's bed?"

"For my kid's bed, yeah, I do, because he moves all over
the place at night. And his closet is already a mess, and what
does he care . . ."

"What about you, Maryvonne, you use fitted sheets?"

I take my nose out of my cup.

"Hmm?"

"You dreaming or what? We're talkin' sheets here. Do you use fitted sheets or don't you?"

"Well, as long as I have a bed to sleep in, that's all I care about."

A woman who works in another shop walks into the canteen.

"Oh, hey, look, you guys. Have you seen how fat she's gotten?"

"That's right, sweetie-pie, she's pregnant."

"I know, but still, she should watch herself. I'd never let myself get that fat. She's gonna have a hard time getting rid of it, I'll tell you that right now."

"Not necessarily, look at me, I gained thirty pounds when I was pregnant. I was a real lardo. But I lost it all again in no time, and without dieting!"

"Well, it's not like that for everybody. Some never get rid of it."

"I swear she's put on at least fifteen pounds and she's only in her sixth month."

"No, not sixth, seventh, she's due the same time as my sister-in-law over in pipes."

"I'm telling you, this is her sixth. She hasn't started her childbirth class yet."

"You want me to ask her? You wanna bet?"

That's how it is every day, morning and afternoon, for fifteen minutes, nothing but yakking. And a little joking around. Just for a change sometime, I'd like to talk about something besides floor wax and lavender-scented laundry detergent. We could talk about our hopes and fears, but no one dares. We don't know each other.

There are days, believe me, when things at the factory just aren't interesting.

And the one time I manage to escape, my thoughts betray me and take me back.

It's nice and cozy here under the covers. I shut my eyes and listen to my heartbeat. My body melts into the sheets, the bed, the whole room. My body is a warm continent with restless rivers running through it. I hear my flesh murmur. I set off to explore. I head upriver and come upon a fantastic land. No towns, no natives in this virgin territory. My hand, a makeshift canoe, drifts over my thighs. I'm all alone. My movements are guided by the rhythm of the blood in my veins. I've hidden my carved silver dagger under the pillow to protect me against wild animals and to sharpen my pencil with. I linger a moment to acquaint myself with a little-known bushy rise. The sun sets here between the trees, and each time it does it sets them ablaze. I have to know more. My arms rub against my breasts. I negotiate my way carefully through this steep terrain, with all its snares.

Lifted on a wave of softness, strong tides catch me by surprise. Inside me, all around me, a vast watery world regulates life. At times, the water rises suddenly, holds steady, and then, just as quickly, recedes I don't know where, and I'm left like a fool rowing on dry land. I should take advantage of high tide to get as far upstream as I can, but the currents, flowing constantly crossriver, make me drift out of control from one bank to the other.

A fruit-bird wheels in the air and dives at me. Its head frightens me. It's as if it's blind. It swoops down at me. I can't get out of the way because I'm being swept along by the current. I scream, "Look out!" It stops in mid-flight. A nasal voice calls back, "Oh, I'm sorry. I'm such a birdbrain, I forgot to look before crossing the stream." He takes off again and I breathe a sigh of relief. My eyes follow him up to the white ceiling.

My eyelids are drooping. It's time to turn out the light.

CHAPTER FOUR

A coffee-colored dawn peeks between the curtains. The darkness takes on a brownish tinge.

"You went back to sleep. You'll be late, Maryvonne, get up!" It's hard to get up every morning, but Mondays are the worst. "Zero energy," as they say. You're even more tired than you are the rest of the week. The thought of starting another whole week back at the grind drains every ounce of strength out of your body. You just want to hibernate.

Sunday night you had a hard time getting to bed. You ran around the house straightening things here and there, setting out your work blues for the next day and the right change for the vending machines. Mindlessly watching the trash on Sunday-night TV, you try to forget that tomorrow is Monday, and you finally go to bed cursing Sunday for never being long enough to enjoy.

The bedraggled workers file into the factory, heads bowed, shoulders slumped, ready to take a beating.

Sometimes, as a kind of gag, when my buddies are around, I walk in backwards. They laugh, but it's not funny.

I open my eyes with a groan. Ready to set myself in motion.

But I'm not at home.

The alarm didn't go off. There isn't any alarm. I've escaped my overseers. I can stretch out and go back to sleep. Bliss.

I don't hear, as I do every morning, the trucks that go rumbling down the street to the port, rattling the windows as they go by. Only the sea birds break the silence. The gray and silvery gulls, the gannets, the terns, the mews, the crested cormorants, and the puffins announce their awakening with a multitude of rising and falling cries. I listen. I can hear again, far away from the machines, far away from the apathy of early mornings with the radio going in the background.

I was going deaf and I didn't even know it.

There are animals at the factory, too, but you don't hear them. Sometimes it's a cat chasing a mouse through the stacks of boxes, sometimes a cockroach scurrying along the pipes, sometimes a snake that has taken advantage of an open dock to slip in under a pallet. Another time you might see a ladybug taking its red cloak out for a stroll on a container. But there's no time to study the life of animals in metallurgy; our own adaptation is enough of a problem.

You get used to the noise eventually, it's true, and as if that weren't enough, as if the noise forced on us wasn't enough to turn us into total zombies, people start hollering, at the top of their lungs, and banging on the containers and the conveyer with their tools. They let off steam in an outburst of gratuitous decibels. Racked nerves become racket makers in these improvised concerts of rage. The foreman, astounded, takes it all in, but doesn't try to stop it, afraid that the violence might be turned on him. Besides, he never plays around, and mostly he's just jealous of our collective music. When the yelling and banging have reached their climax, the din dies down, then out, leaving us all a little dizzy. Everyone goes back to the routine, until next time.

Objects are transformed, too. A rolling flatbed becomes a scooter, a trash can is a hiding place for a bottle of wine, a metal basket turns into a stool, a piece of cardboard becomes a place mat for a snack. Semiclandestine dining areas are set up in corners around the shop and there is feasting in the dust the day before a holiday.

I wake up again later, on my own. The morning light now fills the room. I'm not sleepy anymore. I'm so used to getting up early, either for work or because my son wakes me up, that I can't stay in bed. The thought of hot coffee and croissants makes me jump into my clothes, with no regrets.

I open the door to my room, slowly, without making a sound. It doesn't squeak. I check out the hallway. I'm afraid that that maniac who attacked me yesterday will be there, waiting for me with a cruel smirk on his face. I barely breathe, trying to keep myself from panicking. I shoot across the hall and run down the stairs. I don't turn around, afraid of making the pursuit I dread come true. I don't see anyone. Not even Mrs. Manager.

And what if, like after a catastrophe, I were to find myself totally alone, without another living soul, in this hotel? What if the whole town had been deserted after some alert or disaster I didn't hear in my sleep? What if the entire world were nothing but corpses, ruins, desolation? If I were the sole survivor of a civilization obliterated by some devastating evil? Maybe a nuclear "test" that went haywire and that no one passed but me.

I walk on vapory clouds, a mass of pulsating atoms swarms around me, jeering at me. I feel myself mutating. Green pustules break out on my hands. My hair stands on end. My backup generator is beating like mad in my steel chest.

There's no one in the dining room, either. Yes, there is, there's the waiter over in the corner. I leave my coat and my radioactive imagination on the coatrack. Two tables are still set for breakfast. Mine and that of the couple I overheard talking last night.

I sit down. The waiter walks up, friendly.

"Sleep well?"

"Yes, fine."

"Coffee?"

"With milk, please."

"Croissants?"

"Yes, thank you."

He says only one word at a time, no doubt saving up for his retirement.

I wolf down. Fear makes me ravenous. So does everything else, unfortunately. I'm always hungry, it's the tragedy of my hips. The two from Paris are having breakfast at the same table they ate at last night. I feel like talking to someone. But Jean-François won't be coming.

"Hi, sorry to bother you, but I just wanted to let you know that yesterday, thanks to you, I escaped being raped."

I'm disturbing them. They seem to be at a loss for words.

"Yes, last night as you were coming out of the dining room, I was at the bottom of the stairs trying to fight off this real creep."

They smile politely. Stuffed shirts. And I just stand there. I'm waiting for them to say something. He ventures a response. "Our intervention was purely unintentional. So much the better if we were able to help you, even without knowing it." I forge ahead.

"Are you on vacation?"

Of course they're on vacation, education really pays off when it comes to vacations. I'm on vacation, too. I'll teach them a thing or two.

"I'm a factory worker."

They weren't expecting that. If they keep on staring at me like this, I'll have to tell them that feeding the animals isn't allowed. You'd think workers only existed for them in theory.

One studies their so-called aspirations and historical destiny in books, but one never actually meets any. Can they even talk? One wonders.

He sits there speechless, looking sorry for me. As if to say, "I understand."

He probably pictures me slaving away in an inferno of fire and steel, crawling out of the factory at night, only to go back to my poor family living in some rat-infested hole.

It's a mannerism: he begins speaking, slowly, pronouncing each syllable distinctly to make sure I understand. He's heard and said so much about how terrible working conditions are, and how alienated and dulled workers are by the capitalist mode of production, that he takes me for a dullard.

"Do you work in a poultry abattoir?"

Well, he certainly knows his geography. There actually are chicken farms around here.

"No, metallurgy."

I enunciate distinctly, too, and feel quite proud of my curriculum vitae. At least I make something, at least I know the opposite of "consume."

He goes from surprise to disappointment. To him, metal workers mean Renault and big burly arms and square jaws, kind of apish, like the ones he sees in the May Day parade, working crowd control for the auto workers' union.

Looking up at me, he squints a little. He doesn't have very nice eyes. His lady friend doesn't say anything and thinks I'm imposing on them. She seems to cling to her guru like stringy cheese on a plate of macaroni.

I cut things short: "Well, then, 'bye."

I would have loved to run into Jean-François like that, unexpectedly, and told him that I'm not impressed by the spotless hands of champions-of-the-poor.

I catch a glimpse of myself in the mirror. I'm not in any

shape to meet anybody. I should fix myself up a little. I'll go
have my hair done. Why not change my hair? I can't change
anything else.

I go out. It's cold, an odd kind of cold, which goes right
through me and makes my nipples stand up. Feels like snow.

I make my way through the maze of little streets in the center of town looking for a beauty parlor. Preferably a classy
one, might as well go the whole hog. I won't be any poorer at
the end of the month than I always am. The first one is the
right one.

I push the door, which opens in a flurry of bells. I stand in
the doorway of the shop, done in Louis-the-something style,
like an elephant ready to trample a room full of plaster statu-
ettes. I look so ugly, and I'm dressed so badly. The odor of
marshmallow and ammonia, floating in the close atmosphere,
stings my nostrils. A big sneeze is all I need. I feel so out of
place. I'm getting out of here. Too late. A young woman,
squeezed into tight white jeans, with a professional makeup
job, takes me in hand.

"Good morning, madam, would you like to make an ap-
pointment?"

"Yes . . . uh, no, I mean, if it's possible, I'd appreciate it if
you could take me right away. That would be better for me. I
won't be free otherwise."

"Right now? Well, let's have a look . . . Yes, I think we
could arrange that. What are you having today?"

"A cut . . . and a set."

I don't know what I want, and now I'm stuck. There's no
reason why I shouldn't look good in short hair.

"Chantal, take care of the lady, please."

Chantal in her pink kimono is very young, still learning, no
doubt. She helps me off with my peacoat, as if there were any
need, and hangs it in the closet next to a mink. I put on the

house uniform, a loose overblouse and a terry-cloth towel across my shoulders, and I'm ready for action.

First comes the shampoo. Head tilted back, I surrender. She lathers up my hair, the water is too hot, the back of my neck is killing me. I don't dare say a word. Apparently you do have to suffer to be beautiful, and I have one hell of a handicap to overcome. After she's rinsed me out, Chantal leaves me sitting there to go wash another head. I wait, stoically, in front of the sink. I must be invisible. No one pays any attention to me. I feel ridiculous with this towel wrapped around my head. Despite the thick cloth, water trickles down my neck and runs down between my shoulder blades. A cold gloom comes over me.

After a while, the woman who first approached me and who seems to be the owner of the premises invites me over to a table. I sit facing a wall covered with mirrors which show me just how stupid I do in fact look under my wet hair.

While vigorously combing me out, the hairdresser asks, "How would you like it cut? Blunt, layered, or shagged?"

"I don't know."

I must seem like such a nitwit.

"I'll give you a shag, you'll look very good in it."

"I trust you."

I don't trust her one bit. She brandishes her scissors at my head and starts snipping away. My hair is strewn all over the floor. Oh, well, we'll see what happens. Just relax, Maryvonne.

She's through cutting. My hair is still damp and plastered to my skull. I'm not much better off.

One very dolled-up woman, who got here after me, didn't have to wait as long as I did—a regular client, probably. They cover her head with multicolored curlers that pull the skin of her face back. It makes her look younger. The hairdresser

talks to her about dresses and all the bother women go
through to help out their husbands.

Now it's my turn for a set.

"I'd like something that looks natural."

"Don't worry, sweetheart, it won't be at all sophisticated. I
can see just what will suit you."

Lucky her. I can't see a thing.

Chantal joins her boss, pushing up a little cart filled with
curlers, clips, and bobby pins. The hairdresser gives her
orders in a dry tone.

"Rollers. No, not that one, a bigger one. Bobby pin. Clip.
Medium roller. Roller. Bobby pin. I said medium!" Then, very
sweetly, she addresses herself to me, the client, the patient.
"You'll see, it'll be just lovely."

She flaps around my head, sowing curlers as she goes. She
holds her rat-tail comb between her teeth, adjusts a curl,
stoops down to fix a bobby pin, then stands up on tiptoe,
hands fluttering. She plants herself, legs apart, between me
and the table. Her stomach, squeezed into her pants, is right
in front of my face. I get the urge to run my hand between
her thighs, just to see. I refrain. She goes back behind me and
ends her workout.

"Clip. Quick, Chantal. Net."

She wraps the whole thing in a pink nylon hair net, pulls at
the sensitive hairs still loose at the back of my neck, and
sends me under the dryer to cook.

"Thirty minutes for the lady, Chantal."

"Yes, madame."

Chantal adjusts the temperature and the timer, then puts
me into the oven.

I'm cut off from the rest of the world by the noise and heat
encircling my head. It feels as if my pretty little ears are
roasting. Still going through her contortions, the owner
makes a sign asking if everything's okay. I shake my head as

best I can, what with the rollers knocking against the hood.
I'm on fire, but everything's just fine.

I'm not going to sit here with my hands in my lap like a
schoolgirl off in the corner. A low table in front of me is covered with newspapers and women's magazines. Inside them I
could find invaluable tips on how to look younger, more
beautiful, and more elegant every day. If a woman isn't pho-
togenic, it's because she doesn't want to be. She's guilty of
gross negligence, even worse, of rudeness in the eyes of the
world. Ugly women, hide yourselves, or use Any Old Cream
No. 6. You can do it all: curl, straighten, color, uncolor even
the dullest, most lifeless hair. You can fix those hooked noses
and pointed chins or no chins at all. Who says your breasts
have to sag? Just pick the right weapons to fight cellulite,
fight fat, fight varicose veins, fight stretch marks, fight those
bags under your eyes, fight that blotchiness, fight pollution.
Be a Dream Creation. Don't settle for what nature gave you,
buy the New Naturals. Or else, kiss love goodbye.

I'd rather read the newspaper. I pick up today's *Ouest-
France* and turn to the local news. I stop short as my eyes
catch sight of an intriguing headline:

SHE'S STILL ON THE RUN!

Below that I read:

THE HORRIBLE CRIME OF MARYVONNE T.

Then comes an article which makes me go cold all over.

Our special correspondent went to the scene to try to de-
termine, if not understand, the series of events that
could have made it possible for the no doubt troubled
mind of Maryvonne T. to conceive of such a hideous
crime.

With great difficulty, our special correspondent has

obtained a statement from the devastated family, and has interviewed others close to Maryvonne T. We offer our readers this exclusive report on this disturbing affair.

"Monsieur T., was there anything in your wife's behavior prior to this incident that might have given you any indication that something like this might happen?"

"No, I just can't understand it. We had everything we needed, we were happy. She seemed very attached to the house and her routine. I don't know what to think. Really, I just can't understand it."

"Monsieur T., are you angry with your wife?"

"Yes, of course, I'm angry. You don't just wipe people out like that. I'm suffering a lot. You can understand that, can't you?"

"Monsieur T., would you like to send a message to your wife? If she reads our paper, perhaps she'll see it."

"Yes, I would, thanks. Maryvonne, if you're reading this, I beg you, for your son's sake and for mine, please come back."

The guilty woman's little boy enters the room where the two of us are sitting. A cute little four-year-old, he says, into the microphone, his first cruel words, "Stupid Mommy!" Leaving this ruined family, I went to inquire at the factory where Maryvonne T. works. I questioned her immediate supervisor, a stern but fair man, who told me, "She seemed like a good enough worker. All I can say is she did her work, no more, no less." He added, in a low voice, "She had a tendency to poke fun at discipline."

Her best friend agreed to speak to me about her. "She was my best friend, you know, I like her a lot. Sometimes she had some crazy ideas, but, you know, she was my best friend."

The disturbed personality of Maryvonne T. begins to emerge from these various accounts. Possessing only modest intellectual gifts, undisciplined, eccentric, this

woman who wasn't much to look at had for a long time
suffered from a diminished moral capacity that drove her
to carry out her premeditated crime. A monster had been
hiding behind the wife, mother, and working woman.

Our special correspondent has found out that, still a
fugitive, Maryvonne T. has so far eluded the dragnet set
up by law-enforcement officials. Notify your local police if
you have any information concerning the whereabouts of
the suspect.

I set the paper down. I'm in shock. What a story! I might as
well have killed a traveling salesman, a man with a wife and
family, with a nail file, in a small town on the coast. I might as
well have murdered a man, to be hunted by the police all over
France! It's all a joke: I must have misread it. Despite the intense heat of the hair dryer, I blanch, except for my ears. I
must be mistaken. I pick up the paper again. The article has
been erased. In its place is a series of news items on current
events. A meeting of the Saint-Brieuc association of ex-
alpine chasseurs. A return of a championship to a women's
soccer team from Pordic. The theft of a rearview mirror from
a parked car on Monday night. I feel sorry for the dedicated
journalist who goes to police headquarters to examine the
complaints ledger, hoping for a scoop that never comes.

I'm not in the paper. No one's looking for me. Besides, with
all my new camouflage, no one would recognize me.

The other client, still warm, is being combed out. The curlers are taken out but they leave her hair in stiff coils around
her skull. They look like ball bearings. A few strokes of the
brush change all that. A cloud of hairspray over the whole
thing, and to the approval of one and all, the lady gets ready to
leave. She arrived without a hair out of place and leaves the
same way. I must have missed something. I want to get something for my money.

The thirty minutes are up and I take my head out. I listen.
The hairdresser pats the curlers to make sure they aren't still
damp. That's good. I can't take this much longer. The meta-
morphosis is complete. I'm not kidding, I really look different
with these bouncy layers around my head. Not bad. A new
lease on life!

The last time I was at the hairdresser's was for a wedding—my own. I wanted to focus attention on the upper part
of my body to keep people from looking at my belly where my
baby was already kicking. Everything was done according to
the rules so as to please the emotion-and-champagne-filled
families. We were married in two stirs of the pot and, in the
beginning, it gave me such a thrill just to be putting a cuff on
a pair of men's trousers.

CHAPTER FIVE

I take my new mop for a stroll around Paimpol. The morning is over. If my friends saw me now, they wouldn't recognize me right away.

"Well, look who's back from the repair shop!"

They must be in the cafeteria sawing at a piece of steak "tougher than the butcher's shoe leather."

Each worker occupies his usual place and does so for decades. The conversations also repeat themselves endlessly. They give their opinions of last night's TV movie or of the goings-on around the plant.

"Did you hear that Martandouille was made line foreman?"

"With all the time he's put in sucking up to the bigshots, it's no surprise."

"That makes one more PGPS."

"One more what?"

"One more paid to give people shit."

My place is empty.

"When is Maryvonne coming back?"

"Her husband says this Thursday."

"Short week."

Two days too many. I have no desire whatsoever to go back. They know what's in store for them in the next few hours.

They make the best of this too short moment of rest, till one of
them says:

"No sleeping, it's twenty after. Let's go get some coffee."

They get up, carry their trays back, and go over to the
counter, pushing and shoving to be served on time.

"If the foreman doesn't see us back in the shop on time,
he'll get all bent out of shape. Now we don't want that to happen, do we?"

Day after tomorrow I'll be there with them.

"Oh, girls, if you knew what a wonderful vacation I've had,
you'd die of jealousy."

I wander aimlessly. I look at the shop windows and see my
startling reflection in the glass.

Bam! It hits me. Like a ton of bricks. Who would have
guessed? Here in Paimpol of all places. What a trip! It's incredible, but that's the way it is. Face it. I'm totally lost. I
don't know what to do next. I'm bored to tears. I'm bored stiff.

So stiff I can hardly continue on my little walk to nowhere.
I don't know where to go anymore. I've already been up and
down both sides of this stupid street. Boredom has me by the
throat, I feel like gagging. If it doesn't stop, I'm going to start
crying. I want to go home. I've got ironing piled up, buttons to
sew on. I'll watch the talk shows and game shows on TV.
They're so idiotic, but they'd be perfect today. Mindless vis-
uals, silly stories, trite ideas. Good cheap company, no point
taxing your brain. All you need is a little distraction to keep
you from getting too lonely.

I'll go out to the garden and look over what I've planted. I'll
look to see if the primroses are blossoming. I'll check on how
the leeks are coming along. Those big red tulips I planted last
fall only need the slightest hint of spring to start coming up.
Pretty soon the fragrance of the lilac, the white, the purple,
and the gray will fill my little yard. I'll dote on my crocuses,
which are always so slow to open.

I have quite a green thumb when it comes to flowers. Mine usually open before they die. Vegetables, now that's a different kettle of fish altogether. The fact that they're fated for ratatouille puts me off. Hoeing, weeding, staking, and watering are a bore. I can't seem to absorb "the home vegetable garden in ten easy lessons." I get pointers from people at the factory who come from the country, who used to be truck farmers. Last November, when they told me it was time to plant the noodles, I almost fell for it.

I can't shake these blues hanging over me. My hands, red with shame from being idle, are hiding in my pockets.

If I were at the factory I'd have something to do. My quota. Sometimes, when it's especially high, time goes by too fast. My RHY—required hourly yield—is what I work toward. I work like a demon to pick up the pace. I resist any urge to leave my place. I work out in my head how much I have left before I finish my daily output. I've gotten pretty good at it. The people in my line come to me to do it for them.

"Say, Maryvonne, I punched in at one-forty-five, that's fifteen minutes I have to make up on this lot. I'm supposed to do 54.3 ignitions per hour, how many is that by five o'clock?"

I put down the eight hours and fifty minutes, I carry twenty-five hundredths, add 54.3 ignitions, which I then multiply, I put in the decimal and I come out with the number.

I should enter those Mental Math contests.

It's not enough to just count them though, you've got to do them. I get nervous. A burned-out old guy says to me as he walks by:

"You know what they say, honey, smoking is hazardous to your health."

"So are factories. Just look what forty years have done to you, you old mule."

He walks off muttering.

"Kids nowadays just don't wanna work, all of 'em good for

nothin'. That's why you need bosses, I'm tellin' ya, ya need bosses to give ya ya pay. No work, no pay, and without bosses, no pay, and without . . ."

My friends and I laugh.

"Poor old guy, he's a little slow! . . ."

At certain stations—"the cushions"—the quota is lower. If one of them has the added advantage of a stool, wobbly or not, it's classified as a job for pregnant women. If a man is put there, it almost makes him mad. When I'm given a cushy job, I try to make myself as inconspicuous as I can so I can hold on to it as long as possible. I go full steam ahead, but only so I can slack off and have a snack or go talk to somebody. I go see Beatrice, or she comes over to see me if we're not lucky enough to be working next to each other. We tell each other what's going on with our lives, our worries, our hopes, our husbands.

"You can't imagine, you'd have to be in my position to understand." But we know we understand each other, despite everything. We know when the other has had a bad night by the shadows under her eyes. Flat hair at the end of the month means flat broke. Shaky hands means there was a scene at home. We talk about it and we feel better. But we're pretty hard on each other. If we have something to say, we say it.

"I'm not criticizing you, but I think you're making a mistake if you don't join the walkout."

"Look, Maryvonne, you handled it wrong. You shouldn't have gone to the boss all by yourself. Now he's gonna think we're all just a bunch of jerks."

Sometimes we even get mad at each other, and it takes a while before we make up again. When you like someone, you're hard on them.

What I like most about Beatrice is her nerve, her big mouth. She never gives up. She's thirty-four, that makes twenty years she's worked in the factory, and she's still shouting indignantly, "I don't care, I'm not gonna stay here working like a dog until it's time to retire!"

But there's nothing else on the horizon.

She still wants to believe that pretty soon her ship will come in, that she'll find a nice guy and take a trip around the world. She tells herself that she could be pretty and talk like the women on TV if she wanted. But she knows she's still a long way from shedding her overalls. So she gets riled up.

When I tell her about my little escapade, she'll understand exactly why I did it, and she'll say, "You did the right thing, but look where it got you. When your family name is Unlucky, it's for life."

Outside the factory, in civilian life, we don't see much of each other. We're both caught up in what's called "family life," and when we do see each other, we don't have much to say. Our friendship needs the factory. When we're really down, the factory is a refuge. "You do your work and call it quits." Whereas with your husband and kids, you can never call it quits.

We talk and talk, we make each other feel better, we laugh.

The boss uses our laughter as an excuse to put in his two cents: "So, Maryvonne, I don't want you coming and belly-aching to me about the pace being too stiff. You don't know how lucky you are to be working here. It's a lot worse other places."

"That's so low I can feel it between my toes."

I mean, this isn't a chain gang!

The best times are when there's a stoppage, when the machines break down, or when they run out of materials. There's a long break in the action and nothing to do. The boss announces, real serious, "I know it's hard for you to stop like this, but try to keep your spirits up. I promise you'll be back at it in no time." We all look at each other. Is he kidding or what? Believe me, our spirits are a lot higher when we're not knocking ourselves out. He's the one who's tearing his hair out over his production schedule, not us.

We joke around. We take up a collection for this one guy with long hair so that he can get a haircut. We take up another for this notoriously uptight guy so he can go let his hair down!

Somebody calls my name.

"Hey, Maryvonne! Are these lottery numbers okay? I'd rather check with the union ahead of time, that way I'll know who to blame it on if I don't win!"

I've walked out on all of them. I don't like to think of them sweating away without me, laughing without me. I feel headachy. I could curl up and die the way I must look in this hairdo, in this town where I don't know a soul.

No machine. No friends. No husband. No nothing. I am nothing. I look like nothing. I'm good for nothing. If I fell down, right here on the sidewalk, passed out or dead, people would wonder who would ever come here to die.

I should never have left my rut. Furniture and family are the only life I know. I can always fight it, gripe and complain, but my life is mapped out. I have to come to terms with it. I can cop out and cry over the fact that "Nobody ever helped me, if I had gotten a break, some money, or connections or *something,* I wouldn't be here. If I weren't tied down, I could start over, show some guts, some initiative, different talents, I could be happy."

Let's think straight. I wouldn't be Maryvonne anymore. Maryvonne returns home humbly and waits for her one and only to come home from work too beat to say a word to her.

Come on, Maryvonne, pull yourself together!

You'll be back in the groove with all your machines soon

enough. Your riveting, washing, cooking, and polishing machines. You'll be reunited with all your wrenches, the box, the socket, and the monkey wrench, your hammers, your knives, your screwdrivers, your nuts and bolts, your rivets.

Ease up on yourself.

Okay, I need a good strong cup of coffee. Maybe that will give me an idea about how to finish off my little fling.

It would be easier if I weren't alone.

When I was little I had an imaginary friend who told me stories and played with me. Her name was like music to me and no one was allowed to question her existence. My friend Kakie Célala was my confidante and my inspiration. Kakie Célala went with me everywhere I wanted her to. She made me brave enough to undertake perilous journeys and comforted me in the fall when the hunters shouted and drove me out of my favorite fields and woods. I would tell my mother about all our discoveries, our games and stories. She would laugh, but I'd be the only one blamed for the torn dresses, the lost shoelaces and the stains on my skirts.

Once we made a big decision: Kakie Célala and I were going to move out of the house. All of my mother's attention was taken up with the baby, and my sister, who didn't understand my games, refused to go along with us. So, at the back of the garden, the two of us built a tiny shelter out of rags and old cardboard boxes. Then with the money from my piggy bank we went and bought some bread and chocolate to make sure we'd have something to eat, and hid in our little shack.

A little while later my sister came out.

"I'm s'posed to tell you it's time to eat."

"Who sent you, you little spy, huh, who?"

"Mommy, so there, dummy!"

"Say I'm not here, tell her I disappeared, 'kay?"

My sister shrugged her shoulders and went back into the

house. It started to rain. Slowly but surely our shelter was falling apart. But Kakie Célala and I weren't afraid of bad weather.

"Maryvonne, that's enough! Come in here right now. It's raining and lunch is on the table."

Oh, well, okay, we'll go back, but we'll move out again in the spring.

I have a history of botched escape attempts.

When there are two of you, you're less shy. Kakie Célala and I enter a café.

I order a cup of coffee for myself and a glass of water for Kakie Célala, who doesn't need any stimulants.

Three young imitation rockers are messing around the pinball machine. Their faces, like dolls that grew up too fast, clash with their studded jackets and pointed boots. Kakie Célala nudges me:

"Get a load of this."

They fire off what they say, trying to master rock tempo.

"You catch that fight Saturday night?"

"Negative."

"Those guys from Lanvollon got their asses kicked."

"They act tough, but they were scared shitless."

"I'm not into gang fights."

"You're chicken, man."

"You should'a seen what J.P. did to that tall blond guy. Man, he was bleedin' all over the place."

"Little Louie barfed his guts out. The smell would'a made a rat puke."

"We split just before the cops got there."

"When I go to a dance I take my chick off to a nice dark corner and get to know her. That's what I'm into."

"You get 'em to put out every time?"

"Yeah, ya just gotta lay a good line on 'em."

"You think you're tellin' me somethin' I don't know?"

"I'm just tellin' it like it is."

"Look, I could get as much as I want, but I'm not into chicks, who needs 'em?"

"Man, when you got a nice piece of ass . . . but they gotta keep their mouths shut. Talking turns me off, man."

Kakie Célala and I snicker. They're barely out of kindergarten and they want to play the macho misogynist. That kind of thing isn't made up on the spot, it takes practice.

"What's with you, grandma, you high or what?"

He looks annoyed.

"I'm not laughing because of you. I was thinking of something funny, that's all."

"Okay."

"Hey! Marco, I have to split, the old bag wants me back for slop."

"Me, too, I'm cuttin' out. Later, you guys."

"We're all splittin'. . . . Later."

All three of them leave, rolling their tight little asses. The end.

As for me, I'm staying. I listen to the midday news on the radio. It's past twelve.

The other members of the shop committee have been in a meeting since this morning with the personnel manager. Mr. Chapeau looks like Captain Haddock in the Tintin comics, only less funny. Once a month we do our assembling in the meeting room. The agenda doesn't change much from month to month. At every meeting, the unions present their forty-some-odd demands. They range from salary increases to the installation of a sink to the return of the forty-hour week and improving the quality of the food in the cafeteria. It's maddening. Each point is argued bitterly by the union stewards in front of the personnel manager, who listens with studied indifference. He's just waiting for it to be over. He answers, "No . . . impossible . . . the company can't afford it

. . . not in the foreseeable future . . . we'll deal with that later
. . . under study . . . pointless."

Yet right from the start, we're on the offensive.

"Mr. Chapeau, why don't you tell us straight out what
you're going to let us have today. If you're not going to give us
anything, we'll leave. We don't have time to waste."

The ever-imperturbable Mr. Chapeau responds, "We're
going to examine the issues on the agenda."

He's right. If he were to tell us, "I have nothing to say to
you, you can leave now," which wouldn't be a lie, the out-
raged unions would go crying to the Employee Welfare Board
that management refuses to talk and is threatening the gains
we've made. So, Mr. Chapeau pretends to talk.

One delegate juggles some figures and demonstrates bril-
liantly the continuing fall in purchasing power. It's as if he
believes that all he has to do is express himself well and it'll
somehow work.

"Salaries are increased according to the cost-of-living
index. We have guidelines we have to follow."

"So give us the fifth week of paid vacation and we'll get off
your back."

Maybe if he's caught off-guard he'll cough up.

Waste of breath.

"For the time being it's out of the question. When it becomes a nationwide practice, fine."

We fight for hours over having pollution-control devices
put on the smokestacks releasing toxic fumes.

"Mr. Chapeau, go see for yourself. When birds fly over this
factory they drop out of the sky stone dead. Pfft!"

Gisèle, a newly elected member of the committee, is at-
tending her first meeting. She is stunned. She yawns and retreats into drowsiness. She's taken aback by this powerful
man in the pin-striped suit. She admires her fellow commit-

tee members, so at home in the discussion, who come up with the nerve and the words they need to back the personnel boss into a corner. She feels so out of place, so inept, that she wishes she wasn't there at all. She's disheartened by the boss's arrogance. She wants to see some real change, and they all go on for hours over some window that isn't closing right. Talk about hard work! She wishes she'd never run for the job. Being an activist is too hard, she'll never make it. She thinks about her friends in her line. She thinks how proud she'd be to show them what she can do, because deep down what she'd really like to do is lead a revolt against the whole stinking world.

She'll be able to say so eventually. And not any worse than the others.

Two delegates are screaming at each other over whether or not the shop foreman ordered safety boots. The personnel manager, who never knows what's going on, waits until it's over.

The union secretary solemnly demands that another door be put in the office of the shop committee.

"I don't know why there isn't another door, but there must be a reason. You're not getting a door."

"Look, mister, if you refuse to put in a door, we'll put one in ourselves!"

Idle threats. The personnel manager isn't fazed. They wouldn't dare.

Management's representatives never say anything and sit there looking contrite from beginning to end.

An important issue is raised.

"The X-ray machine is defective. Several lung ailments have failed to be diagnosed during company medical exams."

"We're required to have that machine, we're not required to replace it."

"Mr. Chapeau, you're making a sick joke out of the health of the workers. If the people in this factory heard you, you'd have a revolution on your hands."

The personnel manager smiles. He knows perfectly well that the only thing that will filter out about this meeting is that it was a complete failure, which will put more heat on the union reps than on him. He's not the one who has to face the workers and explain the situation. He does his job. He shows what an understanding, good guy he really is in private discussions with whoever asks for one without going through the union. He always says no, but in such a likable way, which is all it takes to keep up his public image. He does his job and kisses off the rest. The important thing is to stay cool and firm and neutralize the union's influence.

They're talking about promotions.

"How many promotions do you foresee? You know a lot of the men have their skill certification and you're supposed to use them according to their qualifications."

"We'll study the files, there'll be some promotions, how many I can't say."

"And what about the women?"

"Women in Grade One holding technician or mechanic credentials can bid for whatever positions are open."

"You're not answering the question. There are jobs that don't require any technical expertise. That fact notwithstanding, we're requesting that a professional training program be instituted for the women who want it."

"No company's going to do that kind of thing. We're not in business to hand out grants."

When they need unskilled labor, women and foreigners are always the best qualified.

The women who, "according to the maintenance staff, leave their toilets in the locker rooms a filthy mess."

Low blow.

"Mr. Chapeau, may I point out to you that since this meeting began you've left your cigarette butts on the floor, the table, everywhere but the ashtray. So let's not talk about messes."

I can just see him naked. His fat ass and all his flab squished up against his plastic chair. Makes his authority sag some.

In the factory, there's one sort of promotion that isn't negotiated with the personnel manager: election to the shop committee. They put me down on the union list because I have a big mouth and some radical jargon to my credit, and they needed a woman on the committee "to balance things out." I learned that the advantages and duties of a steward set her somewhat apart. The union is really its elected representatives, the "rank and file" are only its supporters. Most people's notion is that to become a shop steward is a responsibility and an honor that you have to prove you're worthy of. You have to be a good lawyer, a good social worker, always courteous, and of good moral character. The union is delegated with the responsibility for the struggle, all demands, personal problems, and discrimination and principles, too.

I have yet to live up to the image of the perfect representative, level-headed and respectable. I fly off the handle. I get impatient. The hemming and hawing of the old guard gets to me. I'm sick and tired of forming pointless delegations to go to the police. If it's true that we have nothing to lose but our chains, I'd just as soon fight it out.

Lenin, with tie and briefcase, is growing impatient beside me. This farce has gone on long enough. Something has to be done if we're ever going to get anywhere. He cups his hands to his mouth to use as a megaphone. He's going to speak. No. He winces and remains silent. A raging toothache is about to make his head burst. It always happens at the wrong time.

His rotting tooth infuriates him, the shooting pain makes him lose his cool. If he speaks, he knows the people around him will smell the stench from his mouth. It's unbearable. He wishes he could curl up in his mother's arms like a little boy. But he's too big for that sort of thing. He roars out, "An end to these Kronstadt fools!"

Meetings put me to sleep. I float above the tables, reclining on a pink cloud, aiming a machine gun loaded with LSD pellets at all of them. I want to see them come out of their shells.

They all let loose. Two fat-bellied management reps fall all over each other trying to unscrew the personnel manager's chair, while another sputters and blubbers as he wipes the dirt off Chapeau's shoes.

Chapeau has tied into a direct link-up with the president's office and listens in on all the juicy details of the latest business junket to Japan. He can see himself, between two gingery meals, sampling the charms of several very talented geishas and an extremely stimulating massage. Chapeau, flushed, feels ready for a position of greater responsibility and a premature ejaculation.

Standing on a chair, one committee member recites the union bylaws. He mimes erotic caresses and now and then whispers, "She's one hell of a dame . . . one hell of a dame. . . ."

Four committee members deal out a round of poker over in a corner. Two others are off in another corner making out. An old-timer who's seen many a strike makes paper airplanes and throws them around the room shouting, "It flies . . . No, it doesn't . . ."

Others have left the meeting room. Whistles, kazoos, horns, laughter . . . a whole parade of workers suddenly appears. Excited, liberated, joyous. "Ladies and gentlemen, the Proletarian Circus, the greatest show on earth."

Ali circles the ring. He has two floor bosses, foaming at the mouth, on leashes, and with a snap of his fingers, he makes them leap through a flaming hoop. The crowd applauds.

Didier solemnly recites a moving poem, and the sound of his voice makes the lights flicker.

Edwige swings high overhead and laughs to see us all so small.

The stains and rips in our work blues have become stars and lace.

Everyone smiles, as if it were true.

Through all the joyful hoopla, certain words come to me, ". . . door . . . locker rooms . . . too small . . . move the union bulletin board . . ."

The shouting keeps me from drifting off. How can they have so much left in them, after ten or twenty years of this? You'd think they were having fun or something.

"For two years now we've been asking for a flashing yellow signal light in front of the factory so we can cross the street without risking our lives."

"They have them over at France Plumbing, regular traffic lights, red, blue, black . . . uh, I mean . . . yellow, blue, green . . ."

In all the excitement, the committee member gets his colored pencils mixed up. The urge to laugh out loud hits me. I can't hold it back. The flustered speaker motions to me to be quiet. My laughter grows and fills the entire room. The more I laugh, the funnier it gets. The personnel manager glares at me. I double over with laughter. To put an end to it, one unionist moves on to the next issue. I go on giggling alone in my corner.

This is never going to end. I've had enough.

"Gentlemen," says Chapeau, "I trust you've noticed that the new showers have been installed."

"Yeah, great, only where's the water?"

Oh, brother! I feel another fit of laughter coming on.

"I wasn't informed of all the particulars. I'll see that it's done, right away."

"Just make sure you hook up the water and not the gas!"

The meeting drags on forever. I'm starving. I'm not coming back, it's just too much.

Rosa's sister sits down at the piano in the drawing room of a beautiful home in Berlin. The bodice of her dress is open to her chest. She takes short little breaths, and notices how white her breasts are as they rise and fall rhythmically. There are more than a million men and women on strike throughout the country. The slender fingers of Rosa's sister busy themselves with a Beethoven symphony. The workers' councils are being organized. The Navy occupies the Royal Palace. What an age! A strand of honey hair, fallen loose from her chignon, dangles over the young girl's forehead. Her eyes narrow slightly as they follow the score. The revolutionary committee has been named. The collapse of the government is at hand. With a graceful gesture, Rosa's sister brushes the stray curl back to join the others. The working classes are on the verge of seizing power. At the piano, the adagios and fugues follow in succession. A sigh lifts the breast of Rosa's sister and dies on the delicately drawn lips. Her supple body sways gently with the melody. Rosa's sister lifts her neck and turns her head slightly, the better to feel the least vibration of the music, as if it were springing forth of its own will. The troops open fire. Repression falls on the leaders of the workers' movement. Rosa's sister's quick fingers leave the keys and rest quietly in her lap. She looks down at the single pearl in her modest ring and the gold bracelet around her wrist. She thinks to herself, "I don't want to be known forever as Rosa's sister!" And she begins playing her piano again, to keep from thinking.

Maryvonne leaves the bistro, finds herself back at the harbor, sits on a bench looking out to sea, takes the novel she began the night before out of her purse, and picks up where she left off.

CHAPTER SIX

I've finished the book. Good work. I'm hungry. I go back to Monoprix. I put two apples in a red plastic basket, required for every purchase. The housewives line up at the registers, their carts loaded with supplies. Rollers stick out from under their scarves. Tapes two feet long come out of the registers at regular intervals. Me and my two apples for one are next. The woman behind me starts dumping the contents of her cart on the belt. Two apples, not exactly what you'd call shopping. I feel pretty cheap. Two apples, one franc seventy-five. I take out my wallet. No, I don't take out my wallet. I look for it: it's not there. But I know I had it, just a few minutes ago, in my purse. I look through my pockets. The customer behind me is getting impatient. The checker, staring out on a panorama of chocolate Easter eggs, drums nervously on the open register. Nothing. I'm so embarrassed I could die. I go through everything again, my purse, my pockets. They remain stubbornly empty. I've lost my wallet. The hausfrau behind me, holding her's in her hand, continues lining up her yogurt, sausages, and bleach. She steps forward, bumps into me and mutters, "People who don't have money shouldn't go shopping."

I have to say something, I can't stand here all day pretending I'm looking for it. The checker goes, "Well?"

"I'm sorry, but I've misplaced my wallet. It's so stupid, I had it just fifteen minutes ago. I'll put the apples back."

"No, stay here. I have to call the manager to cancel the receipt."

She rings the bell next to the register.

All the women trade opinions about this kind of thing and complain about wasting their time. If I at least had had my basket filled with milk, cheese, frozen peas, I would have been one of their own who forgot her wallet at home. Those things happen. But with only two apples, I don't inspire much solidarity.

The manager walks up, annoyed, and snaps at the checker who's bothering him.

"What's the problem here?"

"The lady forgot her wallet. The receipt has to be canceled," she says blandly.

The receipt is signed and stuck in the register drawer.

"No, just leave the apples, we'll put them back."

Confidence reigns.

I leave as fast as I can. The other women proudly pay for their purchases. I guess I won't be having lunch today. Anyway, the whole incident has ruined my appetite.

I retrace my steps carefully, as far as the bench, then back to the café, no sign of a wallet anywhere. This is awful. I don't have a penny left. This sort of thing only happens to me. I hardly ever lose anything. Even the most useless things tend to stick to me like mussels to a rock. But there's a first time for everything. It was bound to happen some day. There wasn't much in it, two or three hours' pay, two or three hundred hand-mounted faucet screws. A pittance and a sore shoulder.

I could have died murdered. I could have met Prince Charming. But to go and lose my wallet in Paimpol, well, it never crossed my mind. It's too mundane, it's of no interest to anyone, not even reporters from *Ouest-France*.

This is cute—penniless in Paimpol. What am I going to do?

A bank heist? Too risky. Pilfer the poor box in some church? Slim pickings, people's faith nowadays is pretty tightfisted. Mug an old lady and take her pension money when she's coming out of the post office? Too sleazy. Turn a trick, a hundred bucks a throw and I'm out of this fix, treat myself to a new wallet and a bus ticket back home? I wouldn't dare. Steal a car? I'd be too afraid of being caught with the goods. There's nothing left to do but roll up in the gutter like a beggar and wait, starving and shivering, for death. Melodrama.

Without much hope, I walk toward the police station to find out if the missing item has been found.

"No, ma'am, no one's turned in any wallets this afternoon."

I expected as much. I've been lost here for twenty-four hours and no one's turned me in, either. If my owner doesn't come for me, in a year and a day I'll belong to Paimpol.

All I have to do is call the factory and ask my husband to come get me. The cop on duty tells me I can use the phone. Yes, but I'd never live it down.

"Hello! Honey? Listen, the dumbest thing has happened. I've lost my wallet and I'm stuck here in Paimpol . . . Yes, Paimpol . . . What am I doing here? . . . Nothing special, walking around . . . Are you mad at me?. . . No, I don't want to leave you . . . I'll explain when I get home . . . Yes, I know you were worried, of course, I'm sorry . . . I'm sorry, sweetie . . . You didn't get any sleep last night? . . . You must be dead . . . I'm really sorry, I don't know what got into me . . . Yes, I understand . . . Won't you forgive me? . . . Yes, I know I'm a little idiot . . . You're coming? . . . Oh, thank you, honey, see you soon . . . I'll wait for you in front of the church." No way!

I'll have to get out of this one myself. For me to go back under those conditions is just putting the noose around my neck. He'd be only too happy if I called him for help. He'd also hold it against me that I wasn't stronger. He'd be furious that all his worrying would have come to such a pathetic end. It would be humiliating for both of us. I'd have to admit everything, my selfish pleasures and my guilty fantasies. He wouldn't understand a thing, he'd just say I was crazy. I don't want to have to say anything.

I've lived these past few hours for myself, and lived them freely, too, no great revelations, no real catastrophes either. Shrouding my brief little trip in silence will only make it more irrational, more upsetting. Even if I never do this again, there will always be this doubt between us. My desire to run away will make him more considerate, more attentive to my moods out of fear that I'll leave again and that maybe next time I won't come back.

Because he's attached to me, me and his slippers, he likes the feel. He never questions himself. He never asks me anything, either, he thinks he knows me inside and out. I would have surprised him at least this once.

Cinderella wanted to go to the ball. Her fairy godmother came to help. But Cinderella lost her glass slipper as she was running from the palace at midnight.

And Cinderella has to hitchhike home.

I stand at the edge of town, in the direction of Saint-Brieuc. It'll be dark soon. I should have waited for a long June day to run away. Winter days are too harsh for dreams. Leaving the factory, you walk out into the dark, you go to bed, then you get up, still in the dark. It's enough to make anybody depressed.

I only thumb cars with women in them. Nevertheless, a truck driver slows down when he sees me, stops and offers me a lift. "No, thanks, I'd rather walk. I only live five minutes from here."

He doesn't believe me, but he doesn't insist, either. He

drives off laughing and blasts me with a cloud of exhaust, right in the face.

It's snowing. My bad knee warned me. No shelter in sight. I pull my cap down to my eyes. There aren't many cars, and by the time the drivers see me with my thumb out it's too late for them to stop. Just my luck. It would have been a lot smarter if I had broken my leg leaving the house yesterday morning. I wouldn't be here acting like a clown on the side of the road. If I weren't such a chicken I'd be rolling along in that truck, with a high, panoramic view of the fields being blanketed in snow. I'm not going to be so choosy any more, I'd get in any car, even one driven by a shady-looking character. I mentally review several karate moves I saw in a movie once.

Finally, a Porsche slows down, is about to stop and then suddenly peels off. I catch sight of two young guys laughing their heads off. Assholes! You think that's funny? I'd like to see you out here! Spoiled brats! Fuckers! Capitalist piglets!

In my indignation I forget to signal the cars going by, and I walk several hundred meters down the shoulder of the road. Their sick little joke gets me fired up. It serves me right, I shouldn't have been standing there looking victimized. I'm not a victim of anything. I'm completely responsible for my actions. Maryvonne is hitchhiking to get home to her husband after going out for a breath of air. It's snowing, and this little misadventure—laughable, when you think about it— doesn't rattle her composure in the least.

And him there thinking of me as some kind of homebody!

I just glow next to my stove. I'm wild about my washing machine. I can't get enough of my mops and brooms. I get such a kick out of planting peas. I adore my four walls and my waxed floors and I can barely tear myself away when I'm forced to accept a dinner invitation. I'm a stay-at-home like my mother.

No, I don't get off on nighttime TV or laundry or the lawn-mower. But he doesn't want to know it. If I had any free time, he wouldn't relish his liberties as much. He'd rather go out alone, he feels younger that way. Sure, I could go with him if I wanted. All I have to do is come up with a babysitter, just like that, at a moment's notice, for the next couple of hours. But in the end, it's not worth the trouble, it's not my idea of fun, and it's not worth going to bed late. He plays up to me with an irresistible imitation of Lee Van Cleef in *Return from Sabata*. And out he goes.

If I should ever happen to be the one going out, it's a big deal. What is there to eat? What time should I put the kid to bed? And then, "What am I supposed to do here all by my-self?" You can do what you always do, sweetheart, read a book or watch TV.

There's nothing deliberate about it, we're liberals in our family, free, equal, and all that. There's just this oppressive atmosphere, a web of little things he says and does, which traps me and keeps me caged.

I love going out, to cafés to talk for hours with friends, to restaurants for dinner, to keep up on what's happening and to see the few good films that make it this far. The theater fas-cinates me. Long walks in the woods or along the beach help me forget weeks of work. I'd be happy to go fishing, or swim-ming, or jogging in the hills too. He knew that back then. Back when? Back never. Boredom quietly crept in to wreck our happy home. Little by little it took over the living room. Then it laid its sticky paws all over the furniture at every hour of the day. Its foul breath stinks up our bedroom, our bed. It sneaks around, gorging itself on our habits, our exhaustion, our despair. It's become fat, bloated, heavy, it crushes us be-neath its repulsive body. When the master of the house is beat, when he's feeling down, I keep out of his way. I don't ask for anything. I keep the kid from making too much noise. "Daddy's tired, sweetie, go play somewhere else." If he's feeling up, he goes out with the boys and treats other people to his good mood. He goes to bed at dawn, and the next day he drags around, hung over, washed out and hostile.

That's all going to change. His beast of burden is champing at the bit. But until it does, I'm going to strike back and stop whining. At the factory I can stand up to the bosses, raise the spirits of the oppressed, fight for what I believe in. And at home I'm supposed to toe the line? I'm supposed to leave all the fight in me under the doormat and slip on my apron without a peep? No way. Something's wrong.

I head back to the home front.

My feet are soaked. I stick out my thumb like I mean it this time. All you have to do in life is look the part.

A car stops. I'm in luck. It's a woman behind the wheel. The backseat is full of kids.

"Are you going toward Saint-Brieuc?"

"To Pordic. Will that help?"

"Yes, it'll get me closer, thanks."

"Get in. Excuse the mess. With the kids, you'd have to clean out the car every day."

I'll say. The floor is covered with stale crumbs, muddy footprints, and candy wrappers. The worn-out seat covers, which are slipping off, do a poor job of hiding the dirty fingermarks on the stretched vinyl.

"Hey, Mommy, who's that lady?"

A little girl, face smeared with chocolate, leans over the seat to inspect me.

"My name's Maryvonne, what's yours?"

She won't return my smile, and gets upset.

"Why is that lady coming with us? Do you know her, Mommy?"

Her big brother who's around seven or eight pipes up.

"She's a hitchhiker. We picked her up to give her a ride because she doesn't have a car."

"Are we taking her home then?"

I reassure her.

"No, I'm not going home with you. I have a house of my own and that's where I'm going."

The mother apologizes.

"They're not used to it. I never pick up hitchhikers. But when I saw you out there in the snow, I told myself it would be inhuman to leave you standing there like that . . . and with a woman, it's not the same, you feel more confident."

"Me too. I was hoping I'd get a ride from a woman. I don't often hitchhike. It's a long story. I spent the afternoon in Paimpol and I lost my wallet. There was no way I could take the bus back."

The little girl looks worried. "Don'cha have a car? Don'cha have any money? Are you poor?" The young woman and I laugh.

The baby, in its car seat, cranes its neck to get a look at me.

"Is it a boy or girl?"

"A boy."

"What a cute little guy!"

What else can you say in the situation? We have a ways to go together, so you have to keep the conversation rolling.

"How old is he?"

"Fifteen months, two days ago."

"They're so cute at that age, they're just discovering everything."

Actually, they're a pain in the neck, whining and into everything.

"Do you have any kids?"

"Yes, a boy. He's four."

That doesn't make us any younger, sister!

Silence sets in. The clock on the dashboard says almost five o'clock.

At the factory all hell is breaking loose around what few sinks there are. All my pals are finishing up the day laughing hysterically and splashing at each other. It takes about ten minutes to get all the filth off their hands. Some bring their own soap and washcloth and start scrubbing before they get to the trickle of boiling hot or freezing cold water coming out of the faucet. "The least they could do is give us another sink, one with water the right temperature, those cheap bastards." As you gain seniority, your calluses harden, your skin cracks, and your fingers get hopelessly misshapen.

"Whaddya expect, honey, that's the life of an artist, you take the good with the bad."

When you've washed your hands and taken your evening pee, you go back to your place and wait for the whistle.

"The last few seconds are the longest of the day."

"I can't believe it! Is that damn clock going backward or what?"

"Maybe the whistle's busted. I'm not gonna sit around here forever."

"C'mon, girls, we're leavin'. It's not that I'm bored or anything, but I gotta get home to my work."

"Look out, there's the boss over in the middle of the shop watching us with his beady little eyes."

"That little rat. I'm sure it's at least two after!"

We always leave our stations a few seconds before the whistle goes off.

The foreman has tried everything to keep us in line. Threats, the bit about safety, the school lectures, like "You're not babies anymore." But nothing works, at thirty seconds and counting, we can't stand it anymore, and we take off.

*   *   *

I get the conversation going again.

"You don't work, do you? Uh . . . I mean you're a house-wife, aren't you?"

"Yes, I stay at home. You too?"

"No, I work in a factory. Not today, but ordinarily at this time I'm still at the factory. Do you like staying at home taking care of your kids?"

"It depends on the day. Taking care of three young kids is a lot of work. My husband isn't any help at all. I don't have any friends. It can get pretty lonely. What about you, do you like working outside the house?"

"It depends on the day."

Nobody likes the factory. You're more or less resigned to it. Some never get used to it and crack, fast, like the young ones who leave after two or three months, or slow, like the veterans whose minds and bodies are burned out on alcohol.

One day, this girl landed in our shop. Everything about her rejected the factory. She was working on an assembly line near mine. She had black hair, too black to be natural, a cakey complexion from too many layers of makeup, and lips that were way too red. She would wear these incredible false eyelashes and intense blue eyeshadow. She had false, fire-engine-red nails and wore pink rouge, and wherever she went she left a trail of cheap perfume that matched the rest.

The men's eyes pop out of their heads and their faces turn red as they crane their necks to follow "Her Highness's" movements around the plant. Her Highness is round in all the right places, probably too round for her own liking, because she never eats anything but grapefruit. Too weak to hold up under the strain, she has dizzy spells. There she is, at eight in the morning, in the middle of the shop, molded into a white suit whose skirt is slit up the sides. Even her shoes, ankle boots with spiked heels, are perfectly white. The other women, scandalized by such brazenness, waste no time bad-mouthing the "slut." But more than anything else it's the white satin turban framing her doll-like face that unleashes their wrath. "Check out Her Highness trying to fit pipe when she can't even fit into her own clothes!" "The way she's dressed I don't know what kind of screwing she's got on her mind."

She kept her outfits spotless and kissed the factory good-bye.

The snow has stopped falling and covers the countryside. You'd think you were in the mountains, where I've never been. Winter sports are too far and too expensive from where I sit. We make do with weekends in the hills of Arrée, mountains to us, whose highest point is all of three hundred eighty meters.

The Alps don't interest me, the overwhelming scale, snow everywhere, ice, no thanks. All in all, ideally, I prefer the golden beaches of the Bahamas, coconut trees in Honolulu, or bougainvillaeas in the Antilles.

Stretched out on the warm sand, I soak up the rays of the sun, softened now and then by a light breeze from off the sea. Time hovers gently. Twilight never ends. The seashells whisper sweet songs. My body, appeased, no longer bothers me. All I care about is my inner life. My arms and legs, my back, my head have all stopped aching. And like a ripe fig drying up on a Turkish terrace, I'm good for nothing. I'm not any uglier than a hippopotamus, so nobody's going to pay to look at me in a zoo. I lie idle, even though, except for yearly vacations, I'm not entitled to. I only exist within the limits of my body. I'm not made of clay. I'm not a statue or a tree. The years don't increase my value, only the number of my wrinkles. In order to exist, I have to exert tons of effort with my body, to

shoulder hours and hours of absence from myself. And yet,
how I long for everything beautiful, gentle, restful, and har-
monious! I am slowly melting into a meditation on soft
caramel.

"I'm making a left, you want me to drop you off here?"

I hurry to get my coat back on. We've reached Pordic. I
have to get out of the warm car and start my hitchhiker number again.

"Yes, you can leave me here, this is great, thanks a lot,
g'bye."

I'm not that far from home any more, ten kilometers at the
most. I'm going home. I have to go home. There's no way
around it. If I get a good ride, I'll be there in twenty minutes.
It's too soon, my trip's not over. I haven't had enough time to
myself. I haven't experienced anything. My fantasies have
only been traveler's tales. I could have sailed off to a foreign
country and started a new life. But it's clear that the ties that
bind me are inside, too. I haven't learned anything, and I'm
returning to home port.

Without rushing. I'll walk. That's that. The powdery snow
sticks to my ankles. I'm treating myself to the hard way back,
it draws out my freedom and justifies it. I knew when I left
that Paimpol would only be a brief interlude in my completely
programmed existence. We apologize for this brief interrup-
tion . . . I broke away so as not to be broken in on for twenty-
four hours. The memory of the pleasurable moments is fad-
ing; reality, cold reality, is coming back to me. I strayed off for
a minute. And I'm not sorry. I needed to break the monotony,
to relax, to tend to myself. I unwound and I feel better.
Sooner or later I'll get that sick feeling in my stomach again. I
may never be able to leave again. I'll sow all my unruly desires in my secret garden. Till the day I can't dream anymore.

Who is this woman wandering the roads?

Where are her long strides taking her?

To her husband waiting for her at home.

What if something's happened to him? What if he had an accident in the car or at work while I was gone?

He's been critically injured and he's dying alone in the hospital. He might even be dead.

After the sleepless night he spent worrying about me, he went to work nervous and exhausted. He forgot to check the safety lock on the press. His hands were shaking. He didn't put the bit into the vise right. He went to straighten it and leaned toward the tool. Accidentally, his elbow hit the "on" switch. The force of several tons crushed his head. Horrible! I'm pierced to the heart. I'm nothing anymore. I'm a widow. The man of my life has been snatched from me by a machine. There was nothing I could do. They have sacrificed my love on the altar of production. Workers have nothing to lose but their chains . . . No use yanking at them, they won't give, and they strangle us the first chance they get.

My eyes cloud over with grief, guilt, anger.

They bury him, without flowers or wreaths, as he would have wanted it. A comrade pays a final tribute to the fallen worker, to the man I loved. I am alone. Terribly. Family and friends weep for one of their own. My little boy sobs at my side without really understanding what's happening to him. There's nothing more for me to do here. I wander off, away from all the pity. I must be crazy. Nothing that horrible could happen, it would be so terrible.

Don't die, my darling, I'm coming, I love you.

I run through the snow, stumble, just miss bumping into a road sign, and slow down to my normal pace again. You're not in your right mind, Maryvonne!

My feet are starting to hurt from all this walking. The way back is hard for the prodigal wife. I drag myself as far as the next milestone—Saint-Brieuc, 4 kilometers—and plop myself down on it.

I assess the situation. I have a noose around my neck, a screw loose in my head, a hole in my stomach, and blisters on my feet. Nothing tragic. It'll all be forgotten soon enough.

I'm going home. It's harder than just being there day after day. It's less obvious. And what if I didn't go home? If I let my momentum carry me right through Saint-Brieuc, then Rennes, then Paris, then all France on foot without stopping? I could start my life over a thousand times and still never really have lived. From the highways and byways I'd be able to see every shade of sunrise. I'd go to the ends of the earth and scatter my past behind me and shed my name. Little by little I would lose all my fears. Footloose, my fancy would be at my fingertips. With the strength of my desire alone, I would overcome all obstacles. I'd come from nowhere and have nothing ahead of me.

I'd learn twenty languages, and I could live just as easily in a Thai village as I could among the Berbers or the descendants of the Incas. In my old age I would tell tales of all my dangerous and thrilling adventures. Malaria and prisons in Bolivia, going down the Nile in a dhow, famines in Asia, the pillaging of the temples at Angkor, and massacres perpetrated by African despots. I'd rumba in Cuba. I'd smoke opium in Hong Kong and hemp in Karachi. I'd throw myself into the arms of an Angolan revolutionary with long, sinewy muscles. I would explore tenderly the gazelle-like body of a young Kabyl girl with blue eyes.

Life in the international fast lane.

Or else I might choose the life of a hermit. A peaceful retreat in Tibet or the mountains of Azerbaijan. A vast desert with nothing but an abandoned sheep pen for shelter, where I would spread out a shabby sleeping bag on the hard ground. I'd live off roots and wild berries. I would renounce, in a spirit of exaltation, all the vanities of this world: money, frantic lei-

sure, the ambiguous pleasures of social intercourse. I would
will away doubtful desires and selfish, mercenary ambitions.
Material possessions will mean nothing to me. Even my body
will become superfluous. Eventually, I'll even throw out my
sleeping bag and sleep out in the cold, stretched out on the
stones.

It's all possible. I've heard about those sorts of things.
Travelers, writers, journalists have described adventures like
that. I'll take their word for it. My life won't be found in any
travel guide and I just have to accept it. More realistic joys
are waiting for me around the bend, on the other side of
that hill.

My son will learn to read. Soon, on nice spring days when
we're off, we'll go on family picnics in the woods in our new
drive-now-pay-later car. The camellias will be in bloom. The
shops in the mall will all have light spring dresses in the windows. I'll treat myself to one. I like being barelegged, but I get
chilled easily. Even in the summer, it's a rare day when the
wind isn't blowing. As I walk, my thighs greedily breathe in
the warm air moving under my skirt. Sitting down, my knees
rub against each other, just for the pleasure of feeling skin
against skin, and squeeze together, tight, until beads of sweat
form between them. I wear my panties loose at the crotch and
let the fragrant breezes flow freely. My modest skirts go down to
my calves and brush against them, swaying gently. In the gardens and fields the tall grass slips between my legs to shame-
lessly stroke the insides of my thighs. My skin, hidden under
my well-behaved skirt, gives, softens, thrills to be free.

In the evenings, we'll make dinner with friends, grilled
fresh sardines and homemade cake. Looking a little further
down the road, I can see vacation coming. In five months
we'll have three weeks off. We'll take the tent, the camping
stove, and our shorts, and head for the great outdoors. We'll

have more time to talk, maybe get to know each other again. With summer's help.

Once, early in June, the sun had turned the factory into a furnace. The sweat was dripping down our backs. There were little pools of it around the workbenches. We were all working in a daze between trips to the sink to cool ourselves down. The dust was stinging our noses, eyes, and throats. You could see it dancing, dense, in the sun's rays pouring through the skylights.

Outside, it was a nice day, the air was filled with the smell of freshly cut grass. The days lingered on until almost eleven o'clock at night.

He came to see me in the shop and whispered to me, "At one o'clock let's get a pass and go to the beach, wanna?" Do I want to? Do I ever!

We left using "official business" as a pretext and fled the factory, singing our heads off in the car. "Those poor saps are still sweating away, they don't know what they're missing." We were missing two afternoons' pay, but it's so little, we weren't missing much.

We lay down next to each other on the beach at Binic. I could feel the sun penetrating every pore of my body. We were both glowing in the heat. His happy cock was swelling under his trunks. The excitement of being there, after our escape, added to the sensuality of the sand sifting through our fingers.

The next day at the factory, our sunburns raised a few eyebrows.

I promise I'll give myself a lot more days like that.

Sitting on the milestone I pile up the resolutions. From now on I'll be strong.

At the factory we have to renew the campaign for a shorter work week. If we could get it down to thirty-five hours, it would be a victory. It would still be too much. Too much exhaustion, too much noise, too much humiliation.

I'll go on shooting off my big mouth until we get more sinks put in. There's no such thing as a small demand, there's only the will not to buckle under.

I'll exercise, watch what I eat, and use a little makeup. I'll read books about history, for self-improvement. I'll think more clearly and positively instead of letting my mind get carried away with fantasy and emotion. When I wake up in the morning I'll pick a subject to reflect on, devote my day to it, and do my quota without getting upset.

I'll be more attentive at union meetings, more active. Too often, I'm afraid of speaking up, of not being understood, of not thinking the right thing. There are times when I end up thinking I don't even have any ideas. I let myself be lulled by the big words of those who know how to debate even if I disagree. I let myself be seduced, reduced.

I'll also need to set aside some time for myself. I'll say, "I'm going out tonight." I won't drive myself anymore. I won't sulk anymore and I won't gripe about piddling little things. I'll be a shining example and h-a-p-p-y.

Is it possible? Could my life really be my own one day?

I'm also going to write to Jean-François. A good letter with a little concrete-analysis-of-the-situation and a lot of warmth. A letter that's flashy around the edges, but sincere at heart. He'll want to see me again. He'll think he's making the first move.

On my lunch break, one day when it's nicer outside than it is inside, and when it's so hard to go back to the grind, he'll be waiting for me at the gate. I'll recognize his slim build and his green eyes from a distance, but I won't let him know I see him right away. I'll act as if nothing were happening, as if I'm just walking back to the factory. As a tease, I'll joke around with my pals so that he sees me laughing. I'll look distant, happy, maybe even desirable. At the last second I'll walk up to him without missing a step. He'll take me aside, away from the gates, away from the zone, and he'll say, "C'mon, we're going to Nicaragua, I need you."

All I'll take is a small suitcase and a Spanish dictionary. We'll catch a plane that same day. Him, cool and collected, me, dazzled but calm. We'll encounter landscapes and faces filled with riches. We'll sleep together without touching so as not to extinguish our desire. He'll love me and I'll be an impassioned heroine . . . heroine, schmeroine!

I won't write. He'd think I was coming on to him. He should be the one to write first. But I'm not on strike anymore and too ordinary. All I'm good for is giving out free newspaper interviews. He signs his name and I go back to my machine. I screw and am screwed. He devotes himself to his big noble principles. The land to the peasants, the university to the students, the factory to the workers. Who wants some stinking factory! I want books and pens just like him, not socialist nuts and bolts.

We're watched all the time. They're all waiting for me. Why do they all want to get their hands on me? They drain the life out of me. I don't want to see anybody anymore. I don't want to be of any use to anybody.

I'm sick of:

"Maryvonne, what have you done with my pants?"

"Mommy, I'm hungry."

"Maryvonne, can you get this pamphlet typed up?"

"Maryvonne, at ten o'clock you're taking Mrs. D's place on the line."

"Maryvonne, will you come with me to see the shop foreman? He doesn't want to give me my vacation in August."

"Maryvonne, don't forget to exchange my shoes at the co-op, I got the wrong size."

"Maryvonne, make sure your husband comes to see me one of these days."

"Maryvonne, what do you use for your french fries, oil or shortening?"

"Maryvonne, what's wrong, you don't look so hot. You all right?"

"Maryvonne, I've had it up to here. How are we ever going to get out of this place?"

Leave me alone. Answer your own questions. Solve your own problems! In the first place, you don't get out of this place. You go in for two months and you're swallowed up for forty years.

For a while, you go on halfheartedly looking for another job. The women wish they could be salesclerks or office workers. It looks better. Sometimes you find yourself dreaming of never working again. Maybe if I concentrate real hard the winning numbers in the next lottery will come to me. 3, 15, 22, 25, 32, 40, and millions I wouldn't even know what to do with. But it's not very likely. If I was meant to be lucky, I'd know it by now.

You can also find someone who'll keep you. I'll divorce my miserable pieceworker and marry some bigshot who's holding all the aces.

YF w/child. Nice looking. Kind. Fun-loving. Seeks man 45–50+ fin sec for long-term relationship. I'll live in a chic villa with a view of the cliffs, and done in period style. I'll treat myself to long, lazy mornings and expensive dresses. I'll participate in social activities, like consumer groups or family planning, just to stay in touch with the real world and to be of whatever use I can. I'll take afternoon classes to round out my education. I'll travel. The guy has a heart attack, croaks on the spot and leaves me the money from his life insurance.

I'll take my ex as a lover and greet him with champagne, for I've never forgotten those good old passionate proletarian days. And so on until I've drunk my fill.

When I'm around fifty, and still in pretty good shape, I'll go back to the factory to see all the old faces again and have a few laughs before I get old myself. I'm being a little cynical but, joking aside, it would take at least a twenty-year vacation.

Like I read on the door of a bathroom stall at the factory, "There are years when you just don't feel like doing anything." But you do anyway. Factory, home, the works. Somehow, you make it through those years, more or less in one piece. You slave away and try to think of something else.

Dreaming is all I know. I don't know any other way out. I don't know which I like better, the city or the country. I act as if I can't decide between a trip around the world and a private hideaway. I'd like to be free, but I can't live without a man and without friends. I think of myself as adventurous and I panic over losing my wallet. I love fashionable women but I despise their parasitic existence and spend my own life in hideous smocks covered with stains.

I ask myself stupid questions. I agonize over things that can't be helped. I make everybody miserable with my lousy attitude, and I want to be treated like a saint. I'm enraged over being stuck in the factory year after year, but I don't dare do anything to get myself out. Learn a skill? How? What skill? Typist? Nurse? None interest me. I only get excited by what's beyond my reach. The problem isn't a hard one to grasp, I know it like the back of my hand—I don't like manual labor.

It would satisfy me to just wait, while limitations slowly become excuses and fantasy becomes gobbledygook, to get old. Not old. Finished, used up, and still with nothing to say, only some babbling about life, not even sad. I'll be at peace, without a memory. My head will tick off the minutes of silence, and my heart, which is just another muscle, will ache for nothing more than rest. I'll roll up and die. It'll be fine. It won't be anybody's fault.

But I'm not there yet. I still have days and years to go. In my own inept way, I'll go on living and I'll go on loving, the man in my house.

I pass the sign for Saint-Brieuc. Saint-Brieuc, its cathedral, its magnificent bay, and its class struggles. The working people of Brittany tell their bosses where to go. Take that!

As I round the bend, my house comes into view, not big, not beautiful, average. The light is on in the kitchen.

My steps get longer. You get attached to your home, our home, my home, when you don't have anywhere else to go. It's where you take the bitter with the sweet. Love, hopeless and never spicy enough, simmers on the back burner. The pot I stew in is my own. I guess I am something of an owner after all. And curled up in bed you feel safe even when there's a storm outside.

He's there. He's waiting for me. He put the baby to bed early and he's trying his best to put together a meal for the two of us. He knows I'm coming back. He can sense my approach. He glances out the window, trying to see through the darkness. I can picture him listening for noises from outside, waiting for me to walk in, anxious despite himself, but all's forgiven.

I open the door slowly.

I walk toward him with a smile. Relieved, he watches my homecoming as if nothing has happened.

All I say is, "I want you."

He takes me by the hand, runs his fingers through my hair, and presses my head against his shoulder.

Rediscovering the warmth of his body, I am overcome, I hold him to me tightly. We don't say anthing. Maybe I shed a tear of joy.

I stroke the back of his neck. He slips his hand under my sweater and raises it slowly to my breasts.

Unbuttoning his shirt, I kiss and nibble at his tiny nipples lost in the down of his chest. He throws his head back and laughs with pleasure.

I kiss his forehead, his eyebrows. He closes his eyes. My lips graze each eyelid. I lick the lobe of his ear. His hand dives down into my pants and cups and coaxes my fickle desire.

I explore the softness under his arm with my tongue. I drink his sweet saliva and swoon at the taste.

With his other hand holding my neck, my head bursts with the thousand ways I want him.

I run my hands down his back, I rub and stroke until I feel his warmth begin to moisten.

One of his fingers spreads open the swollen lips enclosing my vagina.

We're pressed against each other, naked. Our eager bodies will stop at nothing. He picks me up and sits me on the edge of the table. The feel of the cold oilcloth excites me even more.

Easy, slow and easy, he puts his stiff penis, his burning phallus, inside me. I can feel our blood beating in unison, in a strong, controlled rhythm.

I'll draw him down against me. Each single in our mutual pleasure, our arms and legs entwine, we're together like never before.

We wait for each other.

Then our overheated passion bursts deep within us like an immense sun. We kiss, wild with joy. Ready to start again.

Love.

Everything is possible.

I love you.

The door. Here's the door, right in front of me. I don't dare move. I'm paralyzed with fear. In a moment . . .

I put the key in the lock as quietly as I can. My heart is pounding. I push open the door. Not a sound anywhere. I make my way toward the kitchen. Silence. Stillness. Nobody.

A little note scribbled on the table.

"I need a few days' rest to think things over, too. The kid's at your mother's. Love."

The room is spinning.

What's happening to me?

Eyes tearing up. I feel sick.

Quick, a chair.

That fucker! He left without even turning off the light!